"You co
totally out of my mind."

Abruptly, Kyle let her go. "But I'm not going to let it happen. I'd be mad to put us both through that sort of hell. You're a one-man girl—I can see it in your eyes—and a job like mine doesn't allow for permanent relationships."

"You've no idea what I'm really like, what I'm capable of coping with," Carrie whispered.

"It wouldn't work, not with the kind of life I lead. I've already proved that once. And I swore I'd never again make promises I simply can't keep." Again his lips touched the nape of her neck, but only for an instant. "Find someone else!" he said harshly. "It won't—it can't—be me."

A new rule, Carrie thought wryly, and after she'd just learned that love makes it's own rules....

Joanna Mansell finds writing hard work but very addictive. When she's not bashing away at her typewriter she's usually got her nose buried in a book. She also loves gardening and daydreaming, two pastimes that go together remarkably well. The ambition of this Essex-born author is to write books that people will enjoy reading.

The Night Is Dark

Joanna Mansell

Harlequin Books

TORONTO • NEW YORK • LONDON
AMSTERDAM • PARIS • SYDNEY • HAMBURG
STOCKHOLM • ATHENS • TOKYO • MILAN

Original hardcover edition published in 1986
by Mills & Boon Limited

ISBN 0-373-02836-9

Harlequin Romance first edition May 1987
Second printing May 1987

Copyright © 1986 by Joanna Mansell.
Philippine copyright 1986. Australian copyright 1986.
All rights reserved. Except for use in any review, the reproduction or utilization
of this work in whole or in part in any form by any electronic, mechanical
or other means, now known or hereafter invented, including xerography,
photocopying and recording, or in any information storage or retrieval system,
is forbidden without the permission of the publisher, Harlequin Enterprises
Limited, 225 Duncan Mill Road, Don Mills, Ontario, Canada M3B 3K9. All the
characters in this book have no existence outside the imagination of the
author and have no relation whatsoever to anyone bearing the same name
or names. They are not even distantly inspired by any individual known
or unknown to the author, and all incidents are pure invention.

The Harlequin trademarks, consisting of the words HARLEQUIN ROMANCE
and the portrayal of a Harlequin, are trademarks of Harlequin Enterprises
Limited; the portrayal of a Harlequin is registered in the United States Patent
and Trademark Office and in the Canada Trade Marks Office.

Printed in U.S.A.

CHAPTER ONE

THE silver-grey gaze that raked over Carrie was bright with undisguised anger.

'I specifically asked the agency to send me a mature woman, not a damned schoolgirl!' exploded the furious man who confronted her.

Carrie felt her own volatile temper begin to stir. A couple of minutes ago she'd been wallowing in near hero-worship, her legs actually trembling at the thought of coming face to face with this man she'd admired for so long. But where was all that famous charm now? she thought to herself slightly belligerently.

On the television screen it positively oozed out at you, almost overwhelmed you. Was it just a con trick, a big front he put on deliberately to help swell the viewing figures? What a shame if it was. Still, it certainly wouldn't be the first time she'd encountered such a phenomenon. In her three years with the Haversham Secretarial Agency, she'd worked for several well-known people and discovered, to her disappointment, that sometimes a big ego merely disguised a sad lack of talent and a mean, unpleasant nature. Yet somehow she hadn't expected Kyle Allander to fall into this category.

With a small sigh, she ignored her tired, aching body and the uncomfortable heat pouring down on her from the blazing African sun. Drawing herself up to her full height—which, admittedly, was only a rather unimpressive five feet—she forced herself to remain calm, somehow kept her temper strictly under control. After all, she was a Haversham girl, and Haversham girls didn't indulge in fits of temper when clients turned out to be more difficult than expected.

'You requested the agency to send you some-one in their early twenties,' she began reasonably. 'And as I'm twenty-two, I seemed the perfect choice——'

'I asked for someone in their early fifties,' Kyle Allander interrupted her tersely. 'Early *fifties*,' he repeated even more vehemently, as if she were deaf as well as the wrong age.

Carrie shuffled her throbbing feet, wished fervently that she could sit down. She really was very, very tired, why couldn't this unfeeling, self-centred man see that? What she wanted more than anything right now was a hot bath, a refreshing cup of tea and then a couple of hours' sleep. Instead, he was making her stand here in this dizzying heat while he ranted on about her being too young.

'Mr Allander,' she said in what she hoped was a patient yet firm voice, 'I'm sorry if there's been some mix-up over my age, but I assure you that I'm fully qualified and perfectly capable of dealing with whatever work you wish me to do. My shorthand and typing speeds are excellent and I'm quite used to working under difficult conditions and at unsocial hours.'

Those silver eyes swept over her again with unnerving intensity, as if they were noting and recording every physical detail.

'You are also a blue-eyed blonde, Miss Shepherd,' he stated bluntly. 'And in my experi-ence, men tend to find it a little hard to concentrate on their work when there are such distractions around. That's why I try to ensure that any females working with my unit are of mature years and preferably rather plain.'

Carrie was absolutely flabbergasted, could hardly believe that he'd actually just said that. This man was turning out to be totally incredible!

'And does the reverse also hold true?' she responded with heavy sarcasm. 'Should young women only be allowed to work with fat and balding older men? Although I suppose if your theory is taken to its logical conclusion, then men and women shouldn't really be allowed to work together at all. Obviously they can't be trusted to go anywhere near each other without getting completely carried away!'

For the first time, a flicker of amusement showed itself on the dark planes of his face.

'The sexual urge is certainly the oldest and the strongest of all our instincts,' he agreed with unexpected calmness. 'However, complete segregation of the sexes seems a rather drastic—and impractical—way of coping with it.'

'Except where your film units are concerned,' she reminded him rather heatedly.

The taut mouth relaxed a little further, almost curved into a smile, and Carrie felt something suddenly melt inside her. Oh yes, the charm *was* there. He was beginning to use it now, quite deliberately she suspected, to try and soothe her ruffled temper, persuade her round to his way of thinking. How many arguments had he won like this? she wondered. Using just the force of his personality to win his point? Stubbornly she braced herself to resist him.

'You have to understand,' he explained smoothly, 'that a film unit working in the field is a small, self-contained group that has to live together twenty-four hours a day. Often we're filming in very remote corners of the world, cut off from any contact with other human beings for days, even weeks at a time. Under those conditions, there's no room for friction of any kind. Take an attractive woman, put her in the company of a handful of men who won't see any other female for weeks on end, and it's a certain recipe for disaster.'

Carrie didn't even bother to answer but just gave a small snort of disgust. What was the point of trying to argue with a man as bigoted as this one?

He must have mistaken her snort for a stifled yawn because he glanced at her sharply, then frowned.

'You must be tired after your journey. You'd better come inside and freshen up, then have something to eat. Since you'll have to stay overnight at least, we can discuss this later.'

She followed him up a flight of steps into the single-storied, sprawling lodge, which was blessedly cool inside. Simon, the tall, friendly man who'd collected her from the airstrip, had already taken her luggage into the lodge, along with the boxes of supplies he'd picked up at the same time. As she went inside she glanced around, hoping to catch a glimpse of him. He didn't seem to be about, though, so she sighed and trudged along in Kyle Allander's wake, her tired legs having some difficulty in keeping up with his long, easy stride.

At last he stopped and opened a door.

'You can have this room for tonight. There's a bathroom a couple of doors along, but go easy on the water, it's a very precious commodity around here.'

Without another word he turned and strode off, leaving her with the distinct impression that he'd

forgotten about her very existence the instant he'd
turned his back on her.

Carrie walked across the room, kicked off her
sandals, then slumped exhaustedly down on the
bed. Half of her mind was still brooding over that
unexpectedly fraught confrontation with Kyle
Allander, while the other half was crammed full of
the fascinating glimpses of East Africa that she'd
collected during that long, bumpy ride from the
airstrip.

Sun-scorched plains broken only by an occasional oasis of trees or a cluster of granite rocks
surging out of the ground; in the distance the dark
shadows of low, rounded hills, while overhead the
bright blue of the sky had been broken by thick
drifts of cloud, their colour varying from pure
white to dark charcoal. She'd been left with the
impression of a land that was beautiful yet savage,
giving off an aura that was both primeval and
infinitely mysterious. It scared her and yet,
funnily, at the same time there was a flutter of
excitement deep inside her, as if something were
slowly stirring to life.

And it was a fitting background for Kyle
Allander, she admitted with a wry grimace. In an
odd way, he affected her in exactly the same way
as this pagan land. Although she'd have died
before admitting it to a single soul, he aroused in
her that same skin-prickling mixture of fear and
fascination. Although she'd stood up to him and
even held her own during their first explosive
meeting, inside she'd been quivering like a leaf. In
fact, she still felt distinctly shaky. There was
something about those intense silver-grey eyes that
threatened to tear all her self-confidence to shreds.
It was so much more than that, though. There was
something about the man himself that was

unnervingly overpowering. Of course he was tall,
physically powerful, and yet somehow his size had
nothing at all to do with it.

Perhaps it was his face, she mused idly. She'd
seen it so often on television, when he was either
introducing one of his documentary series or
guesting on a chat show, and each time it had had
the same effect on her. Probably on ninety-nine
per cent of the female population, she acknowledged wryly. It was a strange face. With its
strong, prominent features, the dark brows, the
heavy slash of jutting cheekbones and the long,
flexible mouth, by rights it should have been ugly.
And yet it wasn't. In a queer way, it was
intriguingly beautiful. And just as familiar was the
black, shaggy thatch of hair that framed that
remarkable face, always just a little too long as if
he couldn't be bothered to waste time at the
barber's when he could be doing something much
more interesting.

Carrie could still clearly remember her immedi-
ate reaction when Miss Haversham had told her
what her next assignment was to be.

'Kyle Allander?' she'd squeaked in excitement.
'*The* Kyle Allander?'

Miss Haversham had given a wry smile.

'I very much doubt if there's two of them,' she'd
remarked. 'I always get the impression that that
man is very much one of a kind.'

Then Carrie's face had fallen slightly.

'But whenever he wants a temporary secretary,
he always asks for Miss Jefferson.'

Miss Haversham had nodded.

'Miss Jefferson's been with him in East Africa
these last few weeks. Unfortunately, her mother's
had to have an emergency operation and Miss
Jefferson's flown home to nurse her when she

comes out of hospital. I've had a message from Mr Allander asking me to send out another Haversham girl as a replacement.'

Carrie suppressed a small smile. Everyone who worked for the Haversham Secretarial Agency was known as a 'Haversham Girl', even if, like Miss Jefferson, they were well into middle-age. It didn't matter, though. The Haversham Agency was head and shoulders above any other agencies of its kind, with a reputation that was famous and well deserved. Of the dozens of girls who applied to join the agency each year, attracted by the high salaries they could earn and the opportunity to travel while meeting and working for some of the most interesting people around, only a handful were eventually taken on, and even they were put through a gruelling six-month course before they were considered ready to be sent out on their first assignment. Anyone who engaged a 'Haversham Girl' knew that they were getting a secretary of the highest quality and, moreover, one who could be trusted implicitly.

The agency offered both permanent and temporary secretarial help, but Carrie had always asked to be given temporary assignments, liking the excitement of never knowing who she'd be working for in the weeks ahead. And now she was going to get the opportunity to meet Kyle Allander, someone she'd secretly admired for years. Ever since she was a teenager, in fact, and had sat transfixed in front of the television with stars in her eyes as she'd seen that arresting face for the first time, felt a queer tingle pulse up her spine as the sheer strength of his personality had radiated out from the small screen.

A door slammed loudly somewhere in the lodge, bringing Carrie sharply back to the present, and

she wrinkled her nose. Well, here she was—only
Kyle Allander was proving to be a very different
man from the one who'd cast that magic spell over
her from the television screen. She almost wished
that she was safely back in London again.
Almost—but not quite. Kyle Allander might be
turning out to be a grave disappointment, if not a
downright problem, but she certainly didn't want
to leave East Africa without seeing more of this
harshly beautiful land.

With a small sigh, she shut her eyes and tried to
nap, but sleep eluded her. Eventually she gave up
and rolled off the bed again. Her two small cases
stood in the corner, so she quickly unpacked, then
found a cotton shirt and a pair of cotton jeans that
looked slightly less crumpled than the rest. After
fishing around for some fresh underwear, she
padded out of the room and along the corridor,
searching for the bathroom.

She soon found it and was relieved to find
that the plumbing was surprisingly modern.
Remembering Kyle Allander's orders about not
using too much water, she took a very quick
shower, then pulled on her clean clothes. Seeing
her reflection in the small mirror on the wall, she
pulled a face. Hardly glamorous, but at least her
clothes were practical. On Miss Haversham's
advice, she'd dashed around the shops and bought
several cotton tops and pairs of jeans, even cotton
underwear, since synthetic fabrics could get very
sticky and uncomfortable during the heat of the
day. To that she'd added a couple of thick jumpers
as the nights could be quite cool by contrast, a
pair of sunglasses, flat-heeled, rubber-soled shoes,
a large sun-hat, sun-tan cream to protect her fair
skin and a large tube of insect-repellent.

Her new wardrobe was all very basic and she'd

cast a wistful look at her usual silk and lace undies
as she'd packed her cases. She had a very feminine
liking for delicate underwear, but fortunately she
also had enough sense to realise that they were
hardly practical for wearing in the wilds of Africa.

The cotton undies now felt rough against her
skin in comparison to the light webs of silk that
she usually wore, and as she left the bathroom she
wriggled slightly uncomfortably.

'I hope you haven't been bitten by an insect,
Miss Shepherd,' remarked an all-too-familiar voice
just behind her.

Carrie jumped violently. She hadn't heard his
silent approach, and as she rapidly turned round
she was alarmed to find him only inches away.
Good heavens, if he crept up on the animals he
filmed as stealthily as this, no wonder he was able
to get such good close-ups!

'No—no, I haven't been bitten,' she stammered,
totally unnerved by that silver gaze so close to her
own. 'It's just—just that my clothes are new and
they're itching a bit.'

He fingered the sleeve of her shirt, the warmth
of his hand seeming to surge right through the thin
material and burn into her skin.

'Cotton,' he said approvingly. 'Good.'

For an instant she found herself ridiculously
pleased that she'd actually done something he
approved of. Then she hurriedly got hold of
herself again, wiped away the small smile that had
begun to curve her lips.

'Are you hungry?' asked Kyle.

'Starving,' she answered quite truthfully.

'Come and have dinner then,' he invited and she
trotted alongside him as he led her to a room at
the end of the building.

A large picture window opened on to a

magnificent view. An umbrella thorn cast a patch of dappled shade, then there was a stretch of flat, open plain finally broken by a dark patch of trees. And in the background, as always, the low hills in shades of blue and purple, stretching away into the horizon.

'There aren't any animals,' Carrie remarked a little disappointedly.

That faint, heart-stopping smile tugged at the corners of Kyle Allander's mouth.

'There are always animals,' he corrected her. 'It's just that we can't always see them. Very sensibly, they tend to stay in the shade during the heat of the day.'

The door opened and a short, grizzle-haired man came in, carrying a tray of food which he set down on the table. His skin was tanned to the colour and texture of leather, making it quite impossible to guess his age accurately, although Carrie thought he probably wasn't quite as old as he looked.

'This is Fergus,' Kyle introduced him. 'Fergus has been with me ever since I made my first documentary.'

Fergus gave a small grunt in acknowledgment of Carrie's polite hallo, then left the room again.

'Not very talkative, is he?' she commented.

'He may not talk much, but he's absolutely indispensable,' Kyle replied, gesturing to her to sit down at the table, then taking a seat opposite her. 'Whatever I want done, Fergus can turn his hand to it. He's quite unique.'

'Does he also turn his hand to the cooking?' enquired Carrie, staring down at her plate suspiciously.

'It's stew,' Kyle offered helpfully.

Carrie cautiously sampled a mouthful, found

that it tasted far better than it looked, and began to eat hungrily.

'Our supplies are fairly limited, so don't expect *haute cuisine*,' Kyle warned her. 'Meals here are good, but pretty basic. Stew tends to feature on the menu with rather monotonous regularity. It's something you'll just have to get used to.'

Carrie's ears instantly pricked up.

'Does that mean you're going to let me stay?'

He shrugged.

'I don't see that I've got much choice.' He gestured to the wild, desolate scene outside the window. 'Where else am I going to find a competent secretary round here?'

'And you're sure I won't prove too much of a distraction?' she asked demurely.

The silver-grey eyes flashed warningly.

'Don't push your luck,' he growled. 'I'm not known for being tolerant and easy-tempered.'

Carrie found that she could well believe *that*.

'On the other hand,' he went on, 'my bouts of temper never last for very long. If you're going to stay, you're just going to have to learn how to sit them out until I'm my usual charming, easy-going self again.'

This time, she actually smiled.

'Okay,' she agreed, 'now we've got that settled, how about telling me exactly what I'm going to be doing while I'm here?'

He finished eating before finally answering her question.

'As you probably already know, we've been filming a wild-life series, concentrating mainly on endangered species like the black rhinos and wild dogs whose numbers have fallen so drastically over the last decade. The aim of the series is to hammer home to people how vitally important it is that these species aren't wiped out altogether. The trouble is, of course, that the needs of man and the needs of these animals seem to be in ever-increasing conflict. That's why we've also looked at different ways of trying to maintain a healthy balance between the two, suggesting ways that emerging countries can satisfy their economic needs without wiping out their local wildlife population. We've been working on the project for a couple of years now and the actual filming's virtually completed. Apart from Fergus and Simon, the rest of the film unit have left, but I'm staying on for a while to work on the book that will accompany the series. You'll be helping to prepare the final manuscript and typing up my day-to-day notes.'

'Why didn't Simon leave with the rest of the unit?' she asked curiously. 'And where *is* he? I haven't seen him since he drove me here from the airstrip.'

Kyle grinned. 'He's probably in his dark-room. He practically lives in there when he's not actually working out in the field. And as to what he's doing here, he's taking the photographs that will accompany my book. He's also working on a project of his own, a photographic record of the bird-life in this part of Africa. I think he's hoping to find a publisher when we finally get back to England.'

Carrie finished her own dinner, then sat back in her chair and stared at him slightly belligerently.

'Well, if there's only you and Simon and Fergus here now, I really don't see why you made such a dreadful fuss about having me turn up instead of the middle-aged spinster you ordered. I'm hardly likely to cause complete chaos among just the three of you, am I?'

'Five of us,' he corrected her absently. 'There are a couple of research students staying at the lodge, carrying out routine observations on the lions in this area. You probably won't see very much of them, though. They've got their own separate suite of rooms and they're out much of the time, keeping track of the movements of the different prides of lions.'

He got up, ambled over to the door, then paused.

'As to your original question,' he went on in a tone that now had a slight edge to it, 'it's Simon that concerns me. He's a damned good photographer—providing he keeps his mind on the job. I don't want his hands getting the shakes every time you go near him.'

Rattled by his arrogant attitude, she turned and glared at him. 'Don't be ridiculous! We only met each other for the first time today. For all you know, Simon might not even like me.'

His gaze drifted over her speculatively. 'That seems fairly unlikely, considering the over-excited gleam in his eyes as he got out of that Land Rover. However, I'm willing to accept that you weren't deliberately leading him on—and that you won't do so in the future.'

'Thank you very much,' she retorted with deliberate sarcasm.

'Don't mention it,' he replied, completely unperturbed. 'And as for myself, you need have no worries on that score. I like tall, leggy brunettes, not skinny little blondes with baby-blue eyes. Providing you don't get an acute attack of hero-worship where I'm concerned, we'll probably work very well together.' Seeing the dark gleam of pure anger in her eyes, he added, 'There's no need to over-react, Miss Shepherd. I'm simply stating a well-known fact of life. Some people tend to get completely bowled over where television personalities are concerned. They think just because they see them on that small screen, they're surrounded by some peculiar mystique that marks them out from everyone else. That's total rubbish, of course. I'm just an ordinary person doing an ordinary job of work. So long as you don't start getting stars in your eyes, we shouldn't run into any problems.'

'Ordinary' was about the very last word she would have used to describe Kyle Allander, Carrie decided furiously. In fact, most of the words that had raced into her mind were completely unrepeatable. Fortunately, she didn't get the chance to disgrace herself by actually saying any of them out loud because he was already talking again.

'I daresay you're very tired, so I suggest you have an early night. I intend to start work at six o'clock tomorrow morning. Please be ready promptly, I don't want to have to wait for you. Good evening, Miss Shepherd.'

And leaving her still quivering with suppressed temper, he coolly strolled out of the room.

'Oh, this is impossible,' grumbled Carrie, wriggling uncomfortably. 'No one takes dictation under these conditions.'

'Miss Jefferson always managed perfectly well,' Kyle informed her equably. 'And you're not being required to take formal dictation, just jot down odd notes. You can type them up later, when you've some spare time, then I can refer back to them when I come to write the main text of the book.'

'Haven't you ever thought of using a dictating machine?' she suggested, slightly irritably.

'Machines have an infuriating habit of breaking down when you most need them,' he replied. 'Human beings are much more reliable—at least, they're *usually* more reliable,' he added repressively.

There was something in his tone that made Carrie shut up and concentrate on her notepad. It was difficult, though, because she was lying flat on her stomach on a very hard stretch of ground, with her notepad propped up in front of her against a large, flat stone.

They'd been here since just before dawn and at first it had been so dark that she could only take notes with the help of a torch. It certainly hadn't been what she'd been expecting for her first day on this new assignment. Up and ready at six o'clock, as instructed, she'd waited for Kyle Allander to show her to a small office, where she could begin to get on with some work. She'd had no idea why he wanted to start so early, but thought perhaps he found it easier to work while it was still cool. Maybe everyone took a siesta once the full heat of the day began to pound down on them. Well, she was perfectly prepared to go along with that. It seemed a very sensible arrangement.

Disillusionment swiftly followed. Kyle put in an appearance a couple of minutes later dressed, like her, in a loose cotton shirt and jeans with a thick sweater pulled over the top for warmth. It would be a couple of hours yet before the heat of the sun chased away the chill of the night.

Carrie was rather annoyed to find that he somehow managed to look oddly elegant in his casual outfit, while she just felt and, she suspected, looked, completely frumpy. Her hair was scraped tidily back into a ponytail, while her feet were encased in flat, thick-soled sandals. They were just

what the guide-book had recommended as ideal
footwear for this part of the world, but they
definitely didn't do anything for a girl's sex-
appeal, she decided gloomily. Not that it really
mattered, though. Kyle had already made it
perfectly clear that he wouldn't find her sexy even
if she'd been wearing the world's most outrageous
négligé. Not that she *wanted* him to find her sexy,
of course she didn't! All the same, under different
circumstances it might have been fun to see if she
couldn't inch her way under Kyle Allander's thick
skin just a little, bring a hot gleam to those cool,
cool eyes. Only that would be a very dangerous
game to play, she reminded herself hastily. And one
that she had absolutely no chance of winning
anyway, not while she was dressed like this as
frump of the year!

Kyle ran a swift eye over her outfit, then nodded
briefly.

'At least you've got the sense to wear something
suitable,' he commented. 'Come on.'

Expecting him to show her to her office, she
padded after him, then blinked with astonishment
as he strode out of the lodge, down the steep steps
and over to the Land Rover.

Scuttling to keep up with him, she pulled at his
sleeve.

'Where are we going?'

He turned and sighed slightly impatiently.

'Miss Shepherd, I'm writing a book about
animals. To do that, I have to watch them, study
them, for days, weeks, even months, both day and
night. I need to know their breeding patterns, what
they eat, where they live, how they hunt, what
kind of relationships they build up with other
members of their species.'

'But—didn't you do all that while you were

filming?' she ventured, suddenly realising that she was woefully ignorant about what this assignment actually entailed.

He gave an even deeper sigh.

'There's no point in the book being a carbon copy of the film. Why would anyone buy it if it were? It has to have a different approach, contain new information, delve into some subjects much deeper than is possible through a purely visual media. Now, will you please hurry? I want to be at the *kopje* before sun-up.'

She didn't want to admit that she had no idea what a *kopje* was and she certainly didn't have the nerve to ask. Instead, she huddled beside him in the Land Rover as he drove it at a nerve-shredding speed across the dark plains, wishing she had a little more flesh on her small, delicate bones to protect them against the jolting and bruising they were getting.

A *kopje* turned out to be one of the outcrops of rock that dotted the plains. This one had a small pool at its foot, and the branches of half-a-dozen trees were etched darkly against the pale velvet of the sky.

Kyle hustled her out of the Land Rover and she stumbled over the rough ground as he manoeuvred her into position behind a low boulder, silently indicating to her to keep quiet. In front of them was a flattened stretch of earth and on the far side, in the shadow of a tall rock, was what looked like a den.

Dawn was approaching fast now, the first fingers of light sliding swiftly into the sky, lending a glimmer of colour to the grey shadows all around them. Carrie hardly noticed, though. Her gaze was nervously fixed on the entrance to the den. What was going to come out of it? Swallowing audibly, her mind flickered anxiously through all the possibilities. Lions, leopards, black panthers—yet did any of the big cats live in dens like this one? She just didn't know. She was about to risk asking Kyle, for her own peace of mind, when there was a rustle of movement at the entrance to the den. Her gaze swivelled back to it in instant alarm and her heart began to pound uncomfortably hard and fast.

A moment later, a small shape wriggled out into the pale light.

'It's a puppy!' she exclaimed in amazement, relief flooding through her at the same time.

Another bounded out to join its companion and Kyle flicked on a small pocket torch so that she could see her notepad more clearly.

'Keep your voice down,' he instructed in a low tone. 'And begin writing. First pup left den at——' he consulted his watch '—at six thirty-five. Second joined it almost immediately.'

He kept dictating and she busily took notes as the scene in front of the den became more busy. The mother dog put in an appearance after the second pup had emerged, a brindled bitch with large, rounded, alertly pricked ears, a short-haired coat and a distinctive white tip to her tail. Three more pups followed her out and they immediately began playfully scrapping with each other, occasionally stopping to try and suckle from the mother dog.

As Kyle fell silent for a few minutes, just watching the antics of the pups, Carrie turned eagerly to him.

'What are dogs doing out here?' she asked.

'Wild dogs,' he corrected her. 'They're a very different breed from the domestic animals you're used to. These dogs hunt in packs, roaming all over the plains, often covering hundreds of miles. They usually stay in one place for a few weeks when one of the females has pups, though.' He spoke almost absently and seemed to be looking for something, his gaze sweeping through the shadows around them before finally fixing on something. 'Ah, there he is,' he said with some satisfaction.

Even though Carrie squinted hard, she couldn't see anything.

'What am I meant to be looking for?' she grumbled softly.

'The leader of the pack,' Kyle told her. He touched her arm lightly, sending a wave of goose-bumps skittering over her skin. Carrie was very glad he seemed quite unaware of her reaction, all of his attention now centred on the small clearing in front of them. Then she saw a male dog moving towards the bitch, bigger, darker, one ear raggedly torn around the edges, the legacy of some old fight. And those eyes! So wild, so devilish!

'I've nicknamed him Satan,' murmured Kyle in an uncanny echo of her own thoughts. He'd moved closer so that he wouldn't have to raise his voice and his breath tickled her neck as he spoke. Quite suddenly, she found it enormously difficult to concentrate fully on the scene in front of them.

'And what have you named the bitch?' she gulped, trying hard to keep her voice perfectly normal.

'Angel,' he answered with dry amusement. 'Because that's what she must be to put up with an old devil like that one.'

The male dog stretched out in front of the den, swatting away a couple of the pups as they jumped over him, trying to coax him to play. Then he closed his eyes, although his ears remained pricked and alert. There was something openly aggressive about his posture even when he was stretched out, half-asleep.

'A typically arrogant male,' remarked Carrie under her breath, with just a touch of indignation. 'Poor Angel, having to put up with a mate like him.'

There was enough light now for her to be able to see the smile that touched Kyle's mouth.

'As a matter of fact, she seems completely devoted to him,' he remarked. 'Some females like being dominated, apparently.' As Carrie instantly bristled beside him, he added, 'Let's do a few more notes,' then he swiftly began dictating again, giving her no chance to respond to his provocative remark.

It was midday when they finally returned to the lodge and by then every bone in Carrie's body ached unrelentingly from lying prone on that hard ground for several hours, feverishly scribbling notes. Yet every minute of it had been absolutely fascinating, and she'd have stayed there for the rest of the day, given half a chance.

Fergus had lunch ready for the two of them. Simon had gone out, apparently hoping to photograph a rare bird that had been spotted by one of the research students yesterday. They ate in silence, Kyle finishing his meal first. He pushed away his plate, then got to his feet.

'You'd better type up those notes this afternoon,' he told her. 'Fergus will show you where to go. And there's some work that Miss Jefferson didn't have time to finish before she had to go back to England. Perhaps you could make a start on that, too.'

After he had gone, Carrie finished her lunch, then stretched her tired limbs. Lord, she was stiff!

What she needed was a long soak in a hot bath to ease all the aches away.

When Fergus came in to clear the table, she gave him a friendly grin, then the thought of that hot bath slid back into her mind again.

'Fergus, where do we get our water from?' she asked curiously.

'There's a small river runs past the back of the lodge,' he told her as he loaded the plates on to the tray. 'Didn't you notice it?'

She shook her head.

'Well, you can't actually see it from the lodge itself, there's quite a dip in the ground there, so the river's out of sight until you're almost on top of it,' he explained. 'We pump our water up from the river as we need it, then it goes through a special purification unit so it's fit to drink and use for washing.'

'I see,' she said thoughtfully.

After Fergus had gone, she got purposefully to her feet. If their water came from a river, then it could hardly be in short supply. She'd no idea why Kyle had been so insistent that she shouldn't use it—unless he enjoyed making people live under spartan conditions—but now that she knew the truth, she saw no reason at all why she shouldn't indulge in the luxury of a bath. It wouldn't take long, half an hour at most, then she'd get on with that wretched man's typing.

Going along to her room, she rummaged around for a towel and some clean clothes, then fished around in a drawer until she found the one small luxury item she'd brought with her. A large bottle of very expensive, beautifully scented bubble bath.

Marching back to the bathroom, she locked the door, ran the taps, and wriggled out of her dusty

clothes. As the hot water gushed out, she poured
some of the bubble bath under the frothing
stream, then smiled with satisfaction as the water
turned a beautiful shade of jade green and a
delicious scent wafted up.

Rather defiantly, she left the taps running for
longer than she'd intended. Then she slowly,
blissfully, lowered herself into the perfumed,
bubble-flecked water.

After a few minutes, she began to feel almost
human again. Her skin was clean, silky soft, and
all her aches were beginning to float away.
Originally, she'd decided to allow herself a ten-
minute soak before dragging herself back to work,
but as the warm water worked its magic on her
tired body, she thought she might be generous to
herself and have a twenty-minute, perhaps even a
thirty-minute soak, instead. Idly, she swished her
hands around, working up a fresh froth of
bubbles, playing with them almost like a child and
feeling completely relaxed for the first time since
arriving at the lodge.

An impatient rattling at the door made her jump
and started her raw nerves twitching all over
again. Annoyed at being disturbed when she was
just starting to feel like her old self again, she
jerked her head round and glared at the unseen
person on the other side of the door.

'There's someone in here!' she yelled irritably,
hoping that whoever was outside would just go
away and leave her in peace. Surely no one else
wanted a bath right at this moment?

To her absolute horror, the door crashed open
and Kyle Allander strode in, his face positively
thunderous.

'I know there's someone in here,' he responded
grimly. 'I heard the water running and I couldn't

figure out what was going on—until it dawned on me that you'd taken it into your head to specifically ignore my instructions about not wasting water. Well, if you insist on behaving like a disobedient child, I'll simply have to treat you like one.'

Then he leant over and, as her eyes opened wide in pure disbelief, he slid his hand into the water and yanked out the plug.

CHAPTER TWO

CARRIE could hardly believe it was actually happening. Absolutely stunned, she sat there like a statue for a few seconds, just watching the water gurgling away down the plug-hole. Then life surged back into her frozen limbs again and with it came a blinding sense of outrage.

'Get out of here, you—you rat!' she gritted.

When he didn't budge an inch, she grabbed the nearest thing to hand—a heavy bar of bath soap—and hurled it at him.

To her disappointment, he ducked it easily. The temptation to have another go and chuck the bottle of bubble bath at him was almost overwhelming, but instead she floundered around beneath the water, frantically searching for the plug. First things first. There was still just enough bubbly green water left in the bath to preserve her sense of modesty, providing she could get the plug back in during the next few seconds.

Realising what she was doing, Kyle brushed her scrabbling hands aside, found the plug himself and then gave a sharp tug, easily snapping the thin chain which secured it to the bath.

'Oh no, you don't,' he informed her tersely as she made a feeble grab at it, and he tossed it over to the far side of the bathroom where it fell on to the tiled floor, way out of her reach.

A howl of disappointment escaped her, rapidly turning to despair as the water level in the bath reached a dangerously low point. Grabbing a tiny

face flannel, she held it in front of her and then
shot daggers at Kyle Allander.

'If you don't get out of this bathroom at once,
I'll—I'll——'

'You'll what?' he enquired cynically. 'Attack me
with that flannel? By the way,' he went on, his
tone taking on an almost lazy note now, 'I
apologise for calling you skinny earlier. I can see
now that you're really not skinny at all.'

As she clutched the skimpy little flannel even
tighter to the generous curves of her breasts, tears
of frustration began to glitter in her sapphire-blue
eyes.

'What are you, some kind of pervert?' she
demanded in a voice that was suddenly humili-
atingly quavery. 'Are you going to stand there and
watch me until I'm quite naked?'

'A lot of men would be tempted,' he agreed with
infuriating calmness, 'but I told you before, you're
not my type.'

'Then why don't you just get out?' she retorted,
noting with fast-mounting horror that only a
couple of inches of water were now left in the
bath.

'Because I don't trust you,' came his instant
response. 'What's to stop you running another
bathful of water as soon as I've left?'

'I won't, I promise I won't,' Carrie burst out.
Oh God, please let him go. The water had almost
gone, she was covered only by a thin froth of
bubbles now and it wouldn't be long before they
melted away. It was a perfectly ridiculous situation
to be in and she hated it—hated *him* for subjecting
her to this humiliation.

'There's only one way to be completely sure that
you don't do any such thing,' Kyle told her,
lounging gracefully against the wall now. 'And

that's to stay here until you've got out of that bath.'

To her horror, she caught herself feeling slightly piqued at the fact that he wasn't even looking at her any more. Instead, he was gazing out of the tiny window, as if the view outside was far more interesting than her naked body. Heavens, she ought to be thoroughly grateful that he didn't find her in the least attractive!

'I can't reach the towel,' she muttered a little sulkily.

He tossed it over to her, still not looking directly at her. Hurriedly, she wrapped it around herself, then clambered out of the bath. Feeling rather more secure now that most of her dripping body was covered by the thick, fluffy towel, she confronted him angrily.

'How did you get in here? I locked the door.'

'The lock can be opened from the outside,' he told her. 'That's something you ought to bear in mind if you've any idea of pulling this little stunt again.'

'All this fuss over a bath,' she grumbled. 'Anyone would think I'd committed a major crime.'

His face altered, darkened, set into an expression that sent a small shiver rippling down her spine.

'Wasting water *is* a crime around here,' he answered grimly.

Carrie tossed her head rebelliously.

'Don't give me that old line again. Fergus told me that we get all our water from the river, so how can there possibly be a shortage?'

The silver eyes turned positively stormy.

'Heaven save me from empty-headed little idiots who come out here thinking they know it all,' he growled, running his fingers irritably through his shaggy black hair. 'Go and get dressed before I'm tempted to put you over my knee and beat some sense into you.'

Carrie was about to spit back that he wouldn't dare when some inner instinct swiftly warned her against it. The trouble was, he *would* dare. This man wouldn't bother to obey all the usual rules of decency. He was a maverick, making up his own rules as he went along. He'd spent so much of his life in wild places that some of that wildness seemed to have rubbed off on him. After all, what civilised man would burst in while she was having a bath and then treat her in such an appalling manner?

'I just wish your television audience could have seen you these last few minutes, then they'd know what you're really like,' she hissed as she dragged the towel tighter around her, then headed for the door. 'I bet your viewing figures would drop to rock bottom.'

Her merely laughed, his good humour returning with unexpected and mercurial swiftness.

'More likely they'd shoot up to record levels,' he mocked her slyly. 'Remember Angel and Satan? It's the devilish streak in a male that females seem to go for. I have enough trouble with women already. I'd have to get a bodyguard to beat them off if they ever found out what a brute I can be when I really put my mind to it.'

Still in a high state of indignation, she was sorely tempted to stay and argue with him, but she felt at a distinct disadvantage while wearing just a towel. Reluctantly, she decided to let it go for now. Anyway, she had a nagging suspicion that he was deliberately needling her in order to provoke a response. He seemed to enjoy a good, stimulating argument, although she suspected that he nearly always won, putting over his own viewpoint with a forcefulness and clarity of reasoning that would be hard to beat.

Padding back to her own room on bare feet, she banged the door noisily behind her, her temper still bristling, then quickly towelled herself dry.

She had just finished dressing when an authoritative rap on the door set her frayed nerves jangling all over again.

'Are you decent?' enquired Kyle's voice.

'Yes, I am—not that you seem to care too much one way or the other,' she threw back at him acidly.

To her annoyance, she heard him chuckle.

'Then come with me—I've something to show you,' he told her.

For a moment she considered a blunt refusal. Then a small sigh escaped her. What was the use? He'd simply barge his way in and drag her out by force. Locks in this place seemed completely ineffective, and the one on her bedroom door didn't look as if it would keep out an eight-stone weakling, let alone someone as physically powerful as Kyle Allander.

She took a couple of deep breaths, arranged a rather haughty, distant expression on her face, which she fervently hoped would disguise the sudden nervousness churning round inside her, then opened the door and stared up at him. Damn it, why was he so tall? He made her feel so *tiny* when he loomed over her like that.

'What do you want?' she asked in a very cool voice.

'Come with me,' he ordered, seizing hold of her arm.

He gripped her so hard that she had absolutely no choice except to scuttle along beside him. One half of her furiously resented his overbearing manner, while the other half noted with some alarm that those long, strong fingers were eliciting a very strange response from her skin, even the flow of her blood, which kept surging to the surface in heated waves. Too late, she wished that she hadn't rolled up the sleeves of her shirt, leaving her arms bare. She'd most definitely have felt a lot more comfortable if there'd been a layer of material between those warm fingers and the ultra-sensitive skin of her arm.

He steered her out of the lodge, then they began to walk away from it, towards the dip in the land that Fergus had pointed out earlier. It was much greener on this side of the lodge, and there were more trees, throwing dark patches of shade. The ground rose gently before finally dipping down again, and as they made their way up the incline, Carrie's nerve-ends abruptly contracted with alarm as she suddenly noticed what he was carrying in his other hand.

'You've—you've got a rifle,' she gulped.

'Of course I have,' he replied, completely unruffled. 'Around here, you should never go anywhere without one.'

Indignation instantly flared up inside her.

'And I thought you were meant to be a conservationist!' she accused. 'How can you possibly justify making programmes about saving wild animals when you walk about carrying a rifle?'

To her surprise, he didn't get equally angry. Instead, he paused for a moment, then pointed towards a thick clump of trees to their left.

'Tell me something,' he suggested conversationally, 'what would you do if a rhino were to come charging out of those trees, heading straight for you?'

Slightly apprehensively, she stared at the dark patch of shadows under the trees, for a moment almost imagining she could see the huge bulk of an animal lurking there.

'I thought you said rhinos were very rare now in this part of Africa,' she parried evasively at last.

'So they are,' he agreed. 'But you might still encounter one now and then. But if you don't fancy a rhino, then how about a leopard? Most of the big cats will go out of their way to avoid any human intruding on their territory, but this leopard has her cub with her and, like any female, she'll ferociously defend that cub against anything she considers to be a threat.'

Carrie swallowed hard and didn't answer right away.

'She's lying in a patch of dappled shade,' Kyle went on softly. 'You don't even see her until you're only a few yards away—and by then it's too late. So—what would you do?'

'Run like hell?' offered Carrie in a small voice.

He didn't laugh at her feeble attempt at a joke.

'You could be an Olympic sprinter and still not be able to outrun any of the big cats,' he warned.

'All right,' she flung back at him irritably, 'I get the message. I pick up the rifle and shoot the leopard. That's what you want me to say, isn't it?'

The silver-grey eyes flared into life.

'No, it is *not*. The rifle's only to be used as a last resort,' he told her tersely. 'If the animal's going to attack and it's obvious you're going to be torn to pieces, then yes, you shoot. But often a warning shot is all that's needed to scare the animal away. Don't ever forget, though, this is still a very primitive land. There's no one around to help if you get into any kind of trouble. Every time you

set foot outside the lodge, your survival rests in
your own hands.'

Subdued, she glanced up at him.

'Have you ever had to kill any animal?' she
asked.

'No, never, thank God. And I hope I never get
into a situation where I have to make that
decision. But I still carry a rifle wherever I go and
I make sure it's always loaded and in good
working order.'

He started walking again and this time Carrie
made sure she stayed very close by his side, every
tree, every bush suddenly seeming a suitable hiding
place for some lurking animal.

'Don't be so jumpy,' he said more gently in a
couple of minutes. 'I didn't want to scare you, I
simply wanted to make you understand that you
don't take any unnecessary chances out here.'

She gave a small, subdued nod, then they
walked on in silence, at last coming to the top of
the gentle rise, where they stopped and gazed
down at the river below them.

Even Carrie could see that it was far below the
level it should have been. There were large
stretches of dried, cracked mud on both banks
where the water-level had dropped, and even the
middle of the river was so shallow that she could
see rocks jutting out above the surface.

'The November rains were very poor this year,'
Kyle told her quietly. 'The water table around here
is at a fairly critical level. I know you're probably
thinking that a bathful of water wouldn't make
very much difference, and in a way you're right.
Yet those few gallons could mean the difference
between life and death to some animal desperate
for water, and it seems to me almost criminal to
squander it on something as inessential as a bath.'

Carrie could feel a sense of shame creeping over her as she remembered how she'd recklessly run that tap for much longer than necessary.

'I just didn't understand,' she mumbled apologetically.

There was so *much* she didn't understand. And that included the man standing beside her, she thought to herself with a strange lurch of her senses. Just when she thought she had him figured out, she caught a glimpse of yet another side of his complex personality and became totally confused all over again. And she definitely didn't like the way she responded so positively to his touch. Of course, it was easily explained—she was probably still suffering from a touch of hero-worship. After all, for years she'd had an adolescent crush on Kyle Allander, secretly drooling over him every time she'd seen him on the television screen. He'd even turned up in her dreams quite a few times, turning them into shamefully erotic fantasies dominated by those enigmatic eyes and that ugly yet beautiful face.

All right, so she was grown up now, but that silly schoolgirl crush was obviously still hanging around somewhere in her system. There was no reason why it should be a problem, though. Now that she'd recognised what was happening, brought the whole thing out into the open, it should be easy enough to deal with it. She lifted her head confidently, quite certain that this was one little fly who wasn't going to blunder blindly into the lethal web of Kyle Allander's powerful sex-appeal.

They made their way briskly back to the lodge. Kyle showed her to a small room that had been converted into an office, then left her there to get on with the pile of typing that was waiting. As she sat down at the desk, she heard the Land Rover starting up outside and sternly stifled a slightly wistful sigh as he drove away, leaving her to pound away at the typewriter for the rest of the afternoon.

He hadn't been joking when he'd said there was plenty of work for her to do. There was the rough draft of the first few chapters of his book to be typed, plus pages and pages of scrawled notes, not to mention the dictation he'd given her that morning. She figured there was several days' work here, and it wasn't going to be made any easier by the fact that Kyle's handwriting was a thick, powerful, almost indecipherable scrawl.

She worked on steadily, asking Fergus if she could have her tea on a tray so she could work on through the evening. Kyle still hadn't returned by the time she tumbled tiredly into bed and she fell asleep while still half-listening for the sound of the returning Land Rover.

Next morning, she was horrified to find she'd overslept.

'Haversham girls are never late,' she muttered irritably under her breath as she pulled on some clothes, dragged a brush through her tangled blonde hair and then rushed out the door.

Hurrying along to the dining room, she found Simon sitting there eating breakfast.

'Coffee?' he offered, holding up the pot.

She glanced at her watch.

'I don't think I've got time. I overslept,' she explained slightly breathlessly. 'And Mr Allander likes to make an early start.'

'Call him Kyle,' advised Simon. 'No point in being formal around here. And you don't mind if I call you Carrie, do you?'

'No, of course not,' she smiled. Simon was really

rather good-looking with his glossy brown hair, dark eyes, and that engaging grin. And there was something in his gaze that told her he didn't find her exactly unattractive either.

'There's no need to rush off. Kyle's already gone out. He left a message to say you were to get on with your typing today.'

'Oh,' she frowned, unable to suppress a small twinge of disappointment. Then she shrugged it off, brightened up. 'Well, in that case I've time for some coffee,' she decided, holding out her cup.

'You know, it's really my fault that you're here at all,' Simon told her as he poured her coffee, then helped himself to a slice of toast.

'How do you figure that out?' she asked curiously.

He grinned. 'Because it was me who sent that message to the Haversham Agency, asking them to send a replacement for Miss Jefferson. Only I misread Kyle's note—you've seen his writing, you know what a terrible scrawl it is. I mistook the figure five for a figure two and asked the Agency to send someone in their early twenties instead of early fifties. I remember thinking it a bit odd at the time because I know Kyle prefers to work with older women. He reckons they're more reliable, cause less trouble. Then I decided he'd just had a change of mind, that he thought a younger person would be better able to cope with the climate and conditions out here.' His grin broadened. 'Anyway, I'm beginning to think it was the most sensible mistake I ever made,' he went on. 'Miss Jefferson was marvellously efficient, but she didn't have beautiful blue eyes and do mad things to my pulse rate.'

Seeing further complications looming on the horizon, Carrie hurriedly tried to switch the subject.

'Where's Mr Allander—Kyle—gone this morning?'

'One of the research students thought he saw rhino tracks downriver this morning. Kyle's gone to check it out, see if the animal's still around.'

Simon's casual statement filled her with alarm.

'Rhino?' she echoed worriedly. 'But aren't they dangerous? What if he finds it and it charges at him?'

'No one's better at looking after themselves than Kyle,' Simon assured her, obviously not in the least anxious. 'Anyway, rhinos are extremely short-sighted. As long as you've got the nerve to stand absolutely still until they're almost on top of you, you can just step aside at the last moment and they'll go charging past. And believe me, Kyle's got that kind of nerve.'

She believed him.

'He certainly seems completely at home in this kind of country,' she commented with a wry twitch of her eyebrows. 'Still, I suppose it's the ideal place for a man who doesn't like women very much.'

At that, Simon let out a great hoot of laughter.

'Kyle not like women? Where on earth did you get that quaint idea?'

'Well,' she wavered uncertainly, 'his general attitude, the way——'

She'd been about to say 'the way he's treated me ever since I arrived here' but just managed to stop herself in time. Just because he seemed totally unmoved by her feminine charms, that didn't mean he responded that way to *all* women. The truth was depressingly obvious. Galling though it was to admit it, she simply didn't turn him on, he wasn't impressed by silky blonde hair, peachy skin and long-lashed sapphire eyes. Other men might find her a knock-out, but she couldn't raise Kyle Allander's temperature by a single degree.

As her self-confidence plummeted to new depths, Simon chattered on, not seeming to notice that she'd gone rather quiet.

'You've got to understand one thing about Kyle. He simply doesn't believe in mixing work and play. Women just don't exist for him while he's involved in the middle of one of his projects. But take my word for it, he certainly makes up for lost time when the project's finally finished. He works hard, but he plays even harder. And he's never short of playmates, either. Mind you, he's only interested in short-term affairs. A few weeks of fun and good times, but once he starts work on his next project then that's it, it's over.'

'And his girlfriends stand for being treated like that?' demanded Carrie with some indignation.

'They don't have a great deal of choice,' admitted Simon with a wry shrug. 'Before they have time to kick up a huge fuss, he's disappeared off to some remote corner of the world and that's the end of it.'

'How very convenient for him!' Carrie snorted. 'With luck, one day some woman will do exactly the same thing to him. It'd be interesting to see how *he* likes being treated like that!'

For a moment, Simon seemed on the point of saying something. Instead, though, he changed the subject and began talking about the photos he'd taken yesterday.

Once breakfast was over, Carrie settled down to work again. She'd hardly made a dent in the huge pile of typing still to be done. By the end of the morning, her fingers were aching from pounding the typewriter and she was beginning to wish that

Miss Jefferson's mother had chosen some other time to be taken ill.

It took her several days to catch up with the backlog of work. At one point she remarked darkly to Kyle that it would have taken her far less time if his writing weren't so appallingly illegible. He'd coolly pointed out that Miss Jefferson had never had any trouble reading it. Then, ignoring her muttered comment that Miss Jefferson was obviously a candidate for sainthood, he'd calmly strolled out and left her to struggle bad-temperedly with a particularly indecipherable page.

Yet despite the odd moments of friction, he often worked companionably alongside her, either dictating notes or revising a chapter section that she'd already typed. An unexpected air of harmony prevailed on these occasions, as if their two minds worked comfortably on the same wavelength, and she rather enjoyed these surprisingly peaceful hours spent in his company.

At the end of the week, Kyle strolled in and unexpectedly asked her if she wanted to go on a short trip with him that afternoon.

'Where to?' she asked brightly, although to tell the truth she'd have been willing to go just about anywhere if it meant a chance to escape from the wretched typewriter for a couple of hours.

'I thought I'd just follow the riverbank for a while, have another look for that rhino Phil reckons is around.'

'Why is it so very important to find just one rhino?' she asked curiously.

Kyle frowned. 'Their numbers have dropped so dramatically that they've almost vanished from this area during the last few years. If one's turned up now, then we need to know about it. Perhaps we can arrange some protection from poachers, even though we're not actually inside one of the National Parks.'

'Poachers?' she repeated, slightly alarmed. 'There are poachers around here?'

The lines of his face deepened, his mouth became hard. 'Where there's big game, there are always poachers,' he answered curtly. 'Some of them are tribesmen, killing the animals for meat. In a way that's understandable because people have to eat and food isn't exactly plentiful around here. But most of them are well-organised gangs who are just after trophies.' His tone sharpened, anger sparked in his eyes. 'They use fast vehicles and modern automatic weapons and they don't give a damn if they wipe a species of animal right off the face of the earth just as long as they can make a profit from their killings. In the case of the rhino, it's the horns they're after. They either sell them to Eastern countries where they're used in traditional medicine, or they're carved into decorative handles for daggers. Dagger handles!' he repeated with frustrated vehemence, a dark flush of colour now showing along his cheekbones. 'They slaughter an animal just for its horn, and for what? To make an ornamental handle that could easily be made from some equally suitable synthetic material!'

Carrie stared at him. He cared, he really cared! It wasn't just an act put on in front of the television cameras to boost the viewing figures for his programmes or sell more of his books. It was something he passionately believed in. He wanted to shake the whole world into awareness, *force* them to realise how dangerously close so many animals were to total extinction, and how man himself, through either greed or plain ignorance, was to blame for their plight.

He gave a slightly embarrassed shrug. 'Sorry,' he muttered. 'Once I get on to the subject of poachers, I tend to get rather carried away.'

'Don't apologise,' she said quickly. 'It's good that someone cares enough to kick up a fuss, wants everyone to know exactly what's happening. It's nothing to be ashamed of, to care about something so deeply.'

One dark eyebrow quirked upwards. 'I'm not ashamed of it. But I don't usually give free lectures on the subject. Come on, let's go.'

Sitting beside him in the Land Rover as it bumped its way slowly along the riverbank, following the winding trail of the river itself, Carrie risked an occasional sideways glance at her enigmatic companion. It seemed to her that the more she knew about him, the *less* she knew about him. The whole situation was very confusing, and her own mixed-up reaction to him wasn't exactly helping. She was beginning to enjoy being with him, suspected that she enjoyed it rather too much for her own good. Yet there was absolutely no point in entertaining any thoughts in that direction. Romance was definitely out. Even straightforward sex was out, although that was something she wouldn't have wanted anyway. She had curiously old-fashioned ideas in that respect. Sleeping around might be fine for some people, yet she instinctively knew that it wasn't for her. So what was left?

Nothing! she decided wryly. Anyway, wasn't she forgetting the number one rule of the Haversham Agency? 'Never get emotionally involved with a client.' Miss Haversham had drummed it into them over and over again, and had a swift remedy for anyone caught breaking the rule—instant dismissal.

Carrie enjoyed her job and didn't want to risk losing it. Rather primly, she inched over to the far end of her seat, as far away from Kyle as she could get.

'Never get emotionally involved with a client.' It was a good rule, a sensible rule. Until now, she had never been tempted to break it.

Until now? She hadn't meant to say that, of course, it had simply been a silly slip of the tongue. Yet she suddenly found herself wishing that she'd stayed in the office this afternoon and got on with her typing. She couldn't get rid of the uneasy feeling that it would have been a lot safer than venturing out into the wilds of Africa with the disturbingly charming and powerful man who sat beside her.

CHAPTER THREE

THEY followed the riverbank for several miles, but without any sight of a rhino. Eventually Kyle steered the Land Rover into a welcome patch of shade and cut the engine. Trees lined the bank for about a hundred yards here, while behind them was a low outcrop of rock.

'We'll climb up those rocks,' Kyle decided. 'It'll give us a better view. Don't forget your sunhat and sunglasses, it'll be hot up there.'

He was right, it was hot. And by the time they reached the top, she was hopelessly out of breath after clambering up the steep jumble of rocks, while she peevishly noticed that he wasn't even panting slightly. Still puffing noisily, she slumped down beside him, ramming her sunhat more firmly on to her head.

'What exactly are you looking for?' she panted as he scanned the horizon through powerful binoculars.

'Anything that's interesting. Sometimes you can sit like this for hours without seeing a single thing. Other days, half the animal population of Africa seems to troop by, as if they're putting on a parade especially for your benefit.'

It soon became pretty obvious that this wasn't going to be a good day. Apart from a few zebra and gazelles grazing in the distance, nothing moved under the heat of the African sun. Kyle didn't seem to care much, though. He looked perfectly relaxed and contented as he sprawled out beside her, his gaze occasionally sweeping lazily

over the panoramic view in front of them, checking
to make sure he wasn't missing anything of interest.

By contrast, Carrie sat bolt upright, not daring
to relax. She just couldn't shake off the unnerving
impression that she was sitting next to an
extremely powerful male animal—and one that
was only pretending to be tame. After a while she
began to find the silence between them slightly
intimidating, so she hunted around for a safe topic
of conversation, then nervously cleared her throat.

'Which do you prefer?' she asked politely.
'Making films or writing books?'

Kyle gave a small groan.

'You sound just like an interviewer on one of
those damned chat shows.'

'If you don't like doing them, why do you
appear on them so often?' she challenged a trifle
indignantly.

'Because they encourage people to watch my
programmes and buy my books,' he answered
promptly.

'Oh, I *see*,' she responded, this time with open
sarcasm. 'So you appear on them because they're
so financially rewarding.'

At that, he uncurled himself and sat up, moving
so close to her that she could smell the fresh,
musky scent of his body.

'If you want to avoid that spanking I threatened
you with once before, don't bait me,' he warned in
a tone that told her this wasn't an empty threat.

Despite the heat, she felt peculiarly cold all of a
sudden, and the nape of her neck tingled most
uncomfortably as the age-old signals of danger
flared into life.

'All right,' she conceded with a mixture of
nervousness and sulkiness, 'so you don't do it for
the money.'

'But I *do* do it for the money,' he purred.

She glared at him fiercely. 'Do you enjoy being deliberately contrary?'

He seemed to consider her question for a few seconds.

'I think that I probably do,' he conceded at last. 'I rather like seeing you get all fluffed up and angry. It makes a nice change from that air of cool efficiency that you put on most of the time.'

Her wayward temper finally got the better of her.

'But I *am* efficient,' she stormed furiously. 'I'm one of Miss Haversham's top girls, I've been assigned to some of her most important clients. I——' She stopped abruptly, shaken by her passionate response. Good heavens, what on earth was happening to her? She'd never let any of her clients provoke her like this before, no matter how difficult they'd been to work for. And some of them had been very difficult indeed, far more so than Kyle Allander. She'd always kept her temper, though, never lost control, been so outspoken. If Miss Haversham ever found out——

'I'm sorry,' she apologised stiffly, 'I spoke out of turn. I shouldn't have said the things I did.'

He relaxed again, lay back and closed his eyes.

'Nonsense. I far prefer it when people are honest. Anyway, it was partly my fault for teasing you. There's actually a perfectly good reason why I want people to watch my films and buy my books—it helps to raise capital to finance future projects. It's as simple as that. The trouble is, the hosts of those damned chat shows aren't really interested in talking about my work, they simply want to ferret around in my personal life.'

Remembering how he always adroitly side-stepped those probingly intimate questions, Carrie smiled involuntarily. 'Perhaps you should have a less interesting private life,' she suggested. 'Then they wouldn't want to know all about it.'

One silver-grey eye snapped open and fixed on her with disconcerting intensity.

'What exactly do you mean by that?'

The question was phrased perfectly politely, so she couldn't understand why a sudden thread of menace seemed to hang in the air.

'Well, I mean——' she faltered, 'that is, you do appear in the gossip columns quite often—it can't be very pleasant for your girlfriends——'

To her relief, that probing eye shut again.

'For your information, it's often those very same girlfriends who tip off the gossip-columnists in the first place. Hasn't it occurred to you, my naïve little Carrie, that they enjoy seeing their photo in the paper, having their names linked with someone who's well known?'

'Then why go out with that kind of girl?'

The question had burst out of her before she could stop it, and now the heat that flushed her skin had absolutely nothing whatsover to do with the blazing rays of the sun overhead.

'My, my, you are an inquisitive little soul, aren't you?' he drawled. 'And I'd have thought the answer to your question was perfectly obvious. I like that type of girl because they know how to have fun. I take it that you do know what I mean by fun?'

She was absolutely scarlet by now. 'Yes, I know,' she mumbled.

'I think I hear a note of censure in that cool little voice,' he commented sardonically. 'Would you like to give me your definition of "fun", Carrie?'

She straightened her shoulders. He'd asked for

it, so he'd get it, she decided furiously, hardly even noticing that he'd called her by her Christian name for the first time.

'Sex without commitment,' she stated very clearly.

Although she didn't dare look at him, she knew that his gaze was fixed on her very firmly again. She could almost feel it boring into her overheated skin.

'Yes, definitely a note of censure,' he murmured. 'You disapprove of the way I enjoy myself when I'm not working.'

Really, this had gone far enough, she decided.

'It isn't for me to approve or disapprove,' came her prim reply. 'I'm merely your temporary secretary. I'm here to help you finish your book and that's all.'

'Such a paragon of virtue,' he mocked. 'I'd be interested to learn how you came to be so much more perfect than the rest of the human race. Tell me all about yourself, Carrie.'

For an instant her mouth clamped shut; she was determined to say nothing at all. Yet all her instincts warned that it wouldn't be very wise to ignore an order from this man, particularly while he was in his present unpredictable mood.

'I'm twenty-two years old and I've worked for the Haversham Agency for two years,' she told him reluctantly at last, in a stiff little voice. 'Before that, I had several different secretarial jobs, but I found them all boring with no challenge in them. That was why I applied to join the agency. Will that do?'

'It most certainly will not,' came his prompt reply. 'I want to know about *you*, not your career. Let's start with your parents. Are they alive or dead?'

'Alive,' she answered with some surprise.

'You've got the advantage over me there. Mine died several years ago,' he admitted in a softer tone. Then, before she could offer any sympathy, he went on, 'Boyfriends?'

'Past or present?' she whipped back immediately.

'Ah, you're getting the hang of the game now,' he grinned approvingly. 'Both.'

'Several in the past, nothing serious. None at the present,' she stated concisely. Then she wondered if she should have admitted that. Perhaps it would have been better to have invented a devoted fiancé waiting for her in England. She'd used that ploy several times before in awkward situations and it had always worked well. Somehow it had never occurred to her to lie to this man, though.

His gaze swept over her thoughtfully, bringing a fresh flush of colour to her skin.

'Now why would a girl like you have reached the age of twenty-two without getting married or having a serious boyfriend?' he mused idly. 'Scared of committing yourself, Carrie? Under that cool exterior is there a timid little mouse who shies away from any emotional involvement?'

'That does it! I've had enough!' she exploded, jumping to her feet. 'I don't have to sit here while you poke your nose into every corner of my private life.'

He gave her an infuriatingly smug grin. 'Tut, tut,' he reproved. 'Haversham girls should never lose their tempers.'

He was right, of course. It was rule number two at the agency, almost as important as rule number one. It didn't matter how difficult, how awkward, how downright impossible a client was, you just had to cope with it as pleasantly as you could and keep smiling, keep smiling, keep smiling...

Carrie tried, she really did, but it was several long seconds before she finally forced the corners of her mouth to curl up in what was more of a grimace than a smile. And to add to her annoyance, Kyle was clearly watching her efforts with some amusement. Sadist! she thought to herself belligerently. It was pretty obvious he was enjoying every moment of this, knowing just how hard she was fighting to keep her simmering temper under control.

'I want to go back to the lodge,' she muttered at last, deciding that she really didn't feel up to coping with this situation any longer. 'The sun's too hot, it's—it's giving me a headache,' she lied.

'Then go and sit in the Land Rover for a while,' advised Kyle. 'I won't be returning to the lodge for another hour or so yet.'

She stamped her foot in frustration.

'But I want to go *now*!' Then, realising with horror that she was beginning to sound like a rather petulant child, she bit her lip, added quickly, 'If you don't want to go back to the lodge yet, then I'll walk. I can't possibly get lost if I follow the river.'

At that, his lazy, almost teasing attitude abruptly vanished. Sitting up, he fixed his eyes on her and she licked her lips nervously as she saw the suddenly stern lines of his mouth.

'Haven't you learnt anything during the few days you've been here?' he demanded, his gaze hard, diamond-bright. 'Or are you just a dumb little blonde after all?' While she was still speechless at this scathing attack, he went on tersely, 'Don't you realise how downright dangerous it is to go anywhere by yourself? I thought

I'd managed to drum that fact into your head,
but apparently I was wrong. Why else would you
be proposing to walk through the bush for several
miles without any protection? For God's sake,
Carrie, you've got a good brain. Use it!'

The fact that he was right, that his basic concern
was for her safety, didn't make his lecturing any
easier to take. Okay, so she'd behaved stupidly,
spoken without thinking, but why couldn't he have
just talked to her reasonably, reminded her
politely that it wasn't safe to walk around on her
own out here? Why did he have to be so
unpleasantly blunt?

Perhaps because he'd known that this was one
way of making certain that she remembered it in
the future, whispered a small voice inside her head.
Obstinately, she ignored it. No, the answer was
much more simple than that. The man was a
savage, she decided in disgust. He'd spent so much
time in the wild places of the world that he'd
reverted back to a caveman mentality.

Yet even that didn't add up. It took someone with
rare insight and intelligence to make those brilliant
documentaries that tugged at the senses and
invariably topped the TV ratings. An insensitive
caveman type just couldn't have done it.

Carrie sighed silently to herself. Kyle Allander
was an enigma that she couldn't even begin to
solve. And right now she didn't even feel up to
trying. All she wanted at the moment was to be on
her own for a while, give her muddled thoughts a
chance to sort themselves out, get back to some
semblance of normality again.

'All right, I'll go and wait in the Land Rover
until you're ready to leave,' she muttered, eager to
seize on any opportunity to get away from him for
a while.

'Don't change your mind and go wandering off,' he warned her. 'I can see the riverbank in both directions from here, I'll soon spot you if you take it into your head to do anything stupid.'

'I'm not an idiot!' she yelled, provoked into another spurt of retaliation. 'Will you please stop treating me like one?'

'Temper, temper,' he reminded her with a lazy grin. Then he added more thoughtfully, 'I'm beginning to think I was wrong about you. You're not a little mouse after all, more like a prickly hedgehog. You're starting to interest me, Carrie. What are you hiding underneath all those sharp spines? Because you are hiding something, I'm sure of it. Do you think I should try to find out what it is?'

Her heart pounding frantically, she turned her back on him, began scrambling down the rocks on legs that were suddenly weak. Damn the man! Why, oh why did his silly teasing affect her like this? And all that nonsense about her hiding something——

Yet was it nonsense? Carrie had known for some time that in a lot of ways she was different from most other girls. It probably all stemmed from her unsettled childhood. With a father in the diplomatic service, she'd travelled all over the world by the time she was in her teens, lived in half-a-dozen different countries, been to a dozen different schools, many of them multi-lingual—and she'd loved every minute of it.

Her nose wrinkled ruefully. At heart she was a gypsy and she knew it. She'd been born with itchy feet, never wanting to stay in the same place for too long. She loved meeting new people, facing new challenges, new experiences. That was why working for the Haversham Agency suited her so well, being sent out on different assignments every few weeks, always on the move.

The trouble was, she wasn't sure she was capable of living a 'normal' life now, settling down in some nice little house in the suburbs with an adoring husband and two point five kids, or whatever the national average was. And that made her feel slightly freaky at times. Despite all the talk of women's lib and equality, somehow everyone still expected girls of her age to want all the things they were traditionally *supposed* to want. She certainly hadn't got anything against marriage, she just couldn't see herself coping with cosy domesticity. Perhaps that was why she'd tended to shy away from any serious relationships—not that there'd really been anyone who'd tempted her to ditch all her reservations and give marital harmony a whirl. Anyway, here she was, twenty-two years of age, and gloomily wondering more and more often if she was destined to finish up a middle-aged misfit.

Clambering down to the foot of the rocks, something made her glance back for a moment. She was rewarded with a fleeting glimpse of Kyle, binoculars clamped to his eyes as he scanned the horizon, still searching for a glimpse of that elusive rhino.

Her pulses seemed to stop altogether for a moment, then catch up with an extra-heavy throb that made her head reel briefly. He scared her. She was ready to admit that now. The trouble was, it was just beginning to dawn on her *why* he scared her. Of all the men she'd ever met, he was the only one who would be a perfect match for her. Another gypsy, someone whose feet and heart were as restless as her own, who would never try to tie her down but would welcome her as a fellow traveller.

Absolutely shattered by the direction in which her thoughts were drifting, she violently shook her head, as if to toss out all the stupid notions that were crammed inside it. What on earth was happening to her? Unless she got a grip on herself, she'd start having romantic daydreams about the two of them wandering hand-in-hand under the African moon—and that really would be enough to make anyone howl with laughter!

You're one of Miss Haversham's most sensible, down-to-earth employees, she told herself firmly. I've no idea what this pagan land's doing to you, but it can just stop right now! You are not—*not*—reviving that silly schoolgirlish crush on Kyle Allander.

Running over to the Land Rover, she pulled open the door, but the heat inside was almost unbearable despite the fact that it had been parked in the shade. Wiping the back of her hand over her damp brow, she glanced round, saw a low, spreading tree near the river's edge. The patch of shade underneath it looked so inviting that she couldn't resist heading towards it. Bearing in mind Kyle's warning, she kept a cautious eye open, but there was no sign of any animals nearby, nothing stirring at all in the heat of the afternoon. Anyway, she was quite near to the Land Rover, she could always dash back and shut herself inside if there was any sign of trouble.

Collapsing under the tree, she stared moodily at the muddy water of the river as it sluggishly flowed by. Her nerves felt completely jangled and she had a dark suspicion that Kyle Allander was somehow responsible for her unsettled state. Too restless to sit still for more than a few minutes, she scrambled to her feet again, then began pacing along the riverbank, trying to walk off her tension.

Apart from the soft gurgling of the water, it was surprisingly quiet. Perhaps that was why she clearly heard the strange little sounds that started to come from behind a thick bush to her left. Funny little growling, mewling noises that intrigued her, made her take a few hesitant steps in that direction, her brows drawing together in puzzlement. Picking her way round the bush, she was confronted with an old log surrounded by tall grass. For an instant, a note of caution sounded inside her head, but her curiosity was fully aroused now and she ignored it. The funny noises were obviously being made by something quite small, so she didn't see how she could possibly be in any danger.

Another couple of yards further on, she parted the long grass in front of her, then her eyes opened wide in astonishment and delight.

'Oh,' she breathed in disbelief as she stared at the source of those strange little sounds. 'Aren't you cute? But what on earth are you doing here, all on your own?'

At her feet a small bundle of fur stirred, rolled on its back and waved surprisingly large paws in the air, as if inviting her to play. The pale gold fur was soft and fluffy, the ears pricked and alert, the pink mouth open in what looked like a welcoming grin, showing small, white teeth.

A lion cub, not much larger than a small domestic cat, a bright ball of mischief that made her grin back with delighted pleasure. About to bend down and tickle the cub's plump little tummy, at the very last instant a shaft of common sense broke through and she abruptly snatched her hand away.

'Carrie, you're being remarkably stupid,' she gulped, in a voice that had suddenly begun to shake. 'Where there are little lions, there are usually big lions. Get away from here, while you still can——'

She'd begun to back away even while she was muttering to herself, her gaze darting frantically around now, seeing the threatening shadow of a lion behind every bush, every tree. Sweat trickled down her spine and her legs felt as if they were melting under her, too weak to support her weight.

'One more step,' she breathed tremulously, trying to encourage herself. 'Come *on*, Carrie, one more step, and another, and another——'

Her voice died away, the breath whistled jerkily out of her lungs. This time there *was* a shadow, she hadn't imagined it, and oh God, the long grass was parting, a sleek shape silently padding out into a patch of sunshine. Then it stopped, froze into stillness, the hard cornelian-like eyes fixed on Carrie with fierce concentration.

A fully grown lioness, panting slightly in the heat so that Carrie could clearly see the sharp, white teeth in those powerful jaws; jaws that any moment now would be closing around her, tearing at her delicate flesh——

Sheer terror tore through her in great juddering waves. It was the stuff of nightmares yet it was real, this lioness now facing her, only yards away, every muscle tensed as the enraged animal made ready to spring. Carrie couldn't scream, couldn't breathe, couldn't move, couldn't do anything except stand there, drenched in fear, praying that it would at least be over quickly, that there wouldn't be too much pain.

Through the thundering of her pulses, she was dimly aware that someone seemed to be calling her name, a familiar voice echoing over and over inside her head. She was way past the stage where she was capable of any response, though. Her horrified gaze was still fixed on the lioness, all her senses fully occupied by the appalling danger that confronted her, her ears registering only the low, throbbing snarl that vibrated in the animal's throat.

Her name came again, spoken more harshly, more insistently. For a split second she thought she recognised the voice; then the lioness took a step forward and something inside her seemed to die.

'Carrie. Carrie!'

Her heavy eyelids briefly flickered, one hand jerked involuntarily.

'You're quite safe, Carrie. Don't panic, just do exactly as I tell you. I've got the lioness covered with a rifle, all you've got to do is back away, but walk slowly, very, very slowly.'

Kyle? Was the voice Kyle's? Yes, it had to be. But he couldn't help her, no one could, the lioness was already gathering together those huge shoulder muscles. Any moment now she'd catapult forward, covering the few yards that separated them in just a split second. Then it would be over, all over——

'Carrie, move!'

Kyle's harsh command sliced through the thick waves of panic that held her glued to the spot. Responding automatically to the authority of his voice, she made a feeble effort to obey him, but it was no good, she couldn't move, her limbs were locked rigid with fear.

'I c-can't,' she stuttered in a voice so faint and shaky that it sounded as if it were coming from miles and miles away.

'Walk, damn you!' Kyle responded in a strained, terse tone. 'I don't want to have to shoot that lioness just because you won't move your legs!'

She tried again, somehow managed to shift one foot a couple of inches; then she took a shuffling step back, like someone in the throes of a debilitating illness.

'That's fine,' crooned Kyle encouragingly. 'Again now, Carrie, come on, keep walking, there's my good girl, just keep backing away, you'll soon be safe.'

His voice was a lifeline, a thin thread that kept her on this side of sanity. She took another hesitant step, then stumbled, almost fell, felt her heart stop beating as the lioness snarled her disapproval, showing all those terrifyingly lethal teeth again. Kyle's voice instantly lapped over her again, deliberately calming her fractured nerves, gently coaxing her to safety.

'Not much further now, Carrie, I'm just behind you, you're almost there. That lioness doesn't want you, she wants her cub, but you're in her way. Once you're out of her path you'll be safe, quite safe, just keep walking, Carrie, I won't let any harm come to you, I promise I won't.'

Step after faltering step, she backed further and further away from the lioness, who was still growling furiously under her breath. Then she felt a strong arm around her waist, the hard, comforting warmth of a man's chest pressing against her back.

'Keep absolutely still,' warned Kyle's voice in her ear. 'And don't make a sound.'

That wasn't hard. She'd absolutely no strength left to move or speak. Only the grip of his arm was keeping her upright, and she slumped weakly against him, gazing at the clearing in front of her with dull eyes.

The lioness was prowling forward again now, but not in their direction. Instead she slunk over to the log, picked the tiny cub up very gently in that fearsome mouth, turned to shoot one last fierce glare in their direction, and then bounded off through the long grass, swiftly vanishing from sight.

Pressed hard against him as she was, Carrie felt the huge sigh of relief that Kyle emitted.

'Well, that's that!' he said almost cheerfully. 'She's taken her cub off somewhere safe, a long way away from us interfering humans. Let's get back to the Land Rover.'

Carrie swayed perilously as he released his grip on her.

'I think I'm going to faint,' she mumbled indistinctly.

His dark brows drew together. 'No, you're not,' he instructed firmly.

At that, a little strength crept back into Carrie's still shaking body. 'Damn it, I'll faint if I want to,' she retorted, her voice shrill with pent-up nervous tension. 'I've just been nearly eaten by a lion, I think I'm entitled to faint, don't you?'

Her brief burst of defiance fizzled out only seconds later. Without any warning, her legs crumpled under her, forcing her to sit down hard on the ground. Huge tears welled up from nowhere, streaming down her face, and she started to shake quite uncontrollably. Expecting Kyle to react with the usual baffled impatience of any male who's suddenly confronted with a fainting, weeping female, instead she gave a small gulp of surprise as he simply sat down beside her, then wrapped his arms tightly around her. It wasn't too difficult to surrender weakly to the impulse to snuggle up close to him, seek comfort in the solid warmth and male strength of his body.

'Hanky?' she snuffled a couple of minutes later as the flood of tears at last began to dry up.

He fished into his pocket and found one. Feeling slightly better, she blew her nose and scrubbed the tears from her face. A little belatedly, she realised she was where a million women would like to be, in the arms of Kyle Allander. There was only one snag, she reflected grimly. She felt—and knew she looked—like a total wreck, red-eyed, tear-stained, bedraggled. So much for romance!

She blew her nose again, finally managed to pull herself together.

'Well,' she sighed ruefully, running her still shaky fingers through her tangled hair, 'I guess that's got to be about the most stupid thing I've ever done in my entire life.'

'You're probably right,' Kyle agreed in a surprisingly reasonable voice. 'No one in their right mind would ever go that near a lion cub. The mother's nearly always very close by, and there's nothing more dangerous on this earth than a mother protecting her baby.'

Carrie shot him a wary glance. 'Why are you being so nice to me?' she demanded. 'I expected you to give me an absolute tongue-lashing, really let rip at me for being so stupid.'

His powerful shoulders lifted in a brief shrug. 'It's not necessary. You're never going to forget what happened today. I could give you half-a-dozen lectures and it still wouldn't make you remember it any more clearly. My guess is that you'll think twice in the future before doing anything like this again.'

She shuddered convulsively. 'I'll have nightmares about it for the rest of my life.'

'Me too,' he confessed grimly.

Surprised, she glanced up at him, was a little shaken by the dark expression that now shadowed his features. 'Why should *you* have nightmares?'

'Why the hell do you think?' he retorted with a scowl. 'Because I feel guilty, of course! I'd no right to let you go off like that on your own, I'd never have done it if you hadn't——'

As he abruptly broke off, she frowned.

'If I hadn't what?' she questioned with growing curiosity.

'Let's just say that I wanted to get you out of my hair for a while,' he growled, his black brows drawing together in a way that warned he'd had enough of this line of interrogation. 'Anyway, about ten minutes after you'd gone, I realised that I should never have let you out of my sight, so I came after you.'

'Thank heavens you did,' she sighed with fervent relief.

There was a pleasant warmth slowly spreading through her now, driving away the last traces of the cold fear that had ripped through her during that terrifying confrontation with the lioness. He was still holding her, although more lightly than he had been before, and she could feel the steady beat of his heart echoing through her body, the rhythm heavy and even, yet growing a little faster—and faster.

The warmth inside her became a soft heat, her skin felt strange, hypersensitive, as if even the touch of her clothes was too much to bear. Overhead, the sun beat down insistently, adding fuel to the queer fire building up inside her, and she began to feel strangely dizzy, disorientated, filled with a sudden longing for—what? Raising one hand in a vague gesture, as if to brush away the odd sensations, her fingers fluttered against Kyle's open shirt-front, for an instant touched skin as heated as her own. He muttered something indistinctly under his breath, his voice unexpectedly thick, and she felt his fingers dig a little deeper into her ribs, leaving marks that would probably deepen into light bruises over the next couple of days.

'I feel—sort of strange,' she whispered in an uneven voice.

She felt him take a deep breath, then another, as if he were suddenly fighting hard for control.

'It's reaction, that's all,' he said at last, rather tightly.

'But I want to——'

Abruptly she stopped, terrified at what her rambling tongue was going to blurt out next.

His breath fanned her neck.

'You want to what?' came his husky prompt. 'To touch me? Perhaps kiss me?'

Carrie swallowed hard.

'C-certainly not!' she denied vehemently, silently praying that he wouldn't detect the lie.

'It's quite natural,' he told her softly. 'It's your body's instinctive response to its recent brush with danger. It wants to celebrate the fact that it's still alive—and what better way than making love?'

At that, she spluttered indignantly, 'I do *not* want to make—make—l-love!' Oh, damn her tongue, why couldn't it say the words without that betraying stammer?

Then a gasp squeezed its way out of her dry throat as he ran his fingertips very lightly over the curve of her breast, pausing for the briefest of moments at the full tip where the betraying hardness of her nipple pulsed against the thin cotton of her shirt.

'I've always been fascinated by body language,' he murmured. 'And your body's talking to mine so very clearly, Carrie.'

Shocked by the deep tug of need that kept

growing and growing somewhere deep inside her, threatening to drag her down into some dark ravishing land where she'd be completely, hopelessly lost, she made a frantic effort to force herself back to reality.

'Body language?' she said brightly, somehow managing to make her voice sound quite casual and detached. 'That sounds fascinating. Do tell me more about it.'

'It's simply a study of the way we communicate with unconscious gestures and physical movements,' he explained, a gently mocking note creeping into his tone now. 'For instance, would you like me to tell you exactly how I know your body wants to make love?'

'Please do,' she answered coolly, fighting desperately to keep all her mixed-up emotions under some kind of control. 'You're entirely wrong, of course, but perhaps you've simply not been studying this body language business for long enough.'

'Perhaps not,' he agreed, the silver-grey eyes glittering now as his gaze locked on to hers, ruthlessly held it. 'Perhaps I imagined the heat of your skin, the flush on your cheeks, the brightness of those blue, blue eyes——'

'Goodness,' she interrupted hastily before he could get on to even more personal details and make her die of embarrassment, 'you sound more like you're listing the symptoms of a common cold.' She glanced at her watch. 'Heavens, is that the time?' she babbled on, 'we really ought to get back, it's nearly tea-time.'

He let go of her as she wriggled out of his arms and hurriedly scrambled to her feet, then he lithely stood up, towering over her.

'Coward!' he challenged softly.

Pretending that she hadn't heard him, she ran on ahead of him to the Land Rover, then huddled on the far edge of her seat as he got in. As he started up the engine, she fervently hoped it wouldn't take them long to get back to the lodge. Quite suddenly, she didn't want to be alone with this man any longer than was absolutely necessary because she'd just discovered a distinctly disturbing fact. She just couldn't trust her own body any more, not where Kyle Allander was concerned. This was the first time anything like this had ever happened to her and she felt completely unnerved. It also dawned on her that the next couple of weeks could be full of deep pitfalls into which she could so easily tumble, if she wasn't very, very careful.

The solution was pretty obvious. Get his wretched book finished and hurry back to England as soon as she could. Perhaps she'd finally begin to feel safe again when there were a couple of thousand miles between them. Yet she had a terrible suspicion that she was never going to feel entirely safe in her life again, not while Kyle Allander existed in the same world as she did. And that uncomfortable thought stayed with her for the rest of the day and kept her restlessly awake for half the night.

CHAPTER FOUR

By morning, she'd finally managed to snatch a couple of hours' sleep. She still felt tired, jaded, a bit shaky from yesterday, but she was thankful to find that at least things seemed to have settled into perspective again. To her utter relief, all those weird thoughts she'd had about Kyle Allander seemed to have floated away some time during the night. He was just her temporary employer, that was all. Those other daft ideas that she'd got into her head were just a reaction to that terrifying encounter with the lioness. Anyone would have felt a bit light-headed after an experience like that. Everything was back to normal again now, even though her nervous system still felt rather bruised and battered after what it had gone through yesterday.

When Kyle joined her and Simon for breakfast, she was relieved to find that her pulses stayed steady, her temperature remained perfectly normal. For his part, he seemed equally indifferent to her. He ate quickly and silently, then got to his feet again.

'You've plenty of typing to be getting on with?' he queried, glancing briefly in her direction.

'Yes, plenty,' she nodded.

'Good. I'll probably be out most of today.'

With that, he strode out of the room. A couple of minutes later she heard the Land Rover starting up, then being driven away at some speed.

Simon looked at her with some curiosity. 'Do I

detect a slight atmosphere between the two of you?' he questioned lightly, lifting one eyebrow.

Carrie cleared her throat rather nervously. 'I did something—well, pretty silly yesterday,' she admitted. 'I'd rather not talk about it, if you don't mind.'

Studying her pale face for a few moments, Simon finally nodded. 'Okay. Do you really have a lot of work to do today?'

'Yes, I'm afraid so,' she nodded. 'Why?'

He grinned. 'I thought you might like to come out with me this morning and keep a lonely photographer company while I go chasing after grey-headed kingfishers.'

It was a tempting offer, but she regretfully shook her head.

'I must get on with the typing, there's loads to do.' She released a rueful sigh. 'Every time I think I've finished a chapter, Kyle takes it away to read it through, then he brings it back the next morning with a great load of alterations and it has to be typed all over again.'

'Kyle's a perfectionist,' agreed Simon. 'I've known him to discard a whole day's filming just because of a tiny flaw that probably no one but him would ever notice. The trouble is, the man's a genius, and all geniuses have to be allowed their little idiosyncrasies. With Kyle, it's an almost obsessive attention to detail. He knows exactly how he wants a finished film or book to look, and he'll move heaven and earth to make sure it turns out exactly as he planned it.'

'Does he run his private life with the same obsessive strictness?' remarked Carrie, half-jokingly.

To her surprise, he took her comment seriously. 'Yes, he does,' he answered with a small frown.

'He allocates so much time for work, so much time for play, and the two are never allowed to overlap. It's the same with personal relationships. They're allowed to go so far, but never any further. He decided years ago that long-term commitments don't fit in with his way of life, so he's simply ruled them out, doesn't allow them to happen.'

Carrie caught the warning undertone in his voice, raised her head and stared at him.

'Are you trying to tell me something, Simon?' she asked a little sharply.

He looked slightly embarrassed. 'I like you, Carrie,' he said simply after a short pause. 'I wouldn't want to see you hurt. There've been a lot of women who've thought they could change Kyle's attitude. None of them ever managed it, though, and none of them ever will. If you want a brief affair and lots of fun, then Kyle's the ideal man for you. But I don't think you're that type of girl. You wouldn't be able to play sophisticated bedroom games without getting badly hurt.'

Hoping that the dull heat building up inside her wasn't revealing itself on her pale skin, Carrie tossed her head defiantly. 'You really are talking a lot of nonsense this morning, Simon,' she scoffed, keeping her voice deliberately casual. 'I'm a Haversham girl, remember? Haversham girls never have affairs with their clients, it's the number one rule of the agency. In fact, they work so hard that they don't usually have time to have affairs with anyone. Now, you'll have to excuse me, I really do have an awful lot of work to get on with.'

With some relief, she escaped to the quiet tranquillity of her small office, where she vented some of her feelings by pounding away on the typewriter with unnecessary force. Why on earth had Simon talked all that rubbish at breakfast?

Did he really think she needed warning about Kyle Allander? Well, he was definitely wrong! This was one girl who knew exactly how lethal the infamous Allander charm could be, and was determined not to let it get to her.

She worked solidly through the day, taking only a very short lunch break, and by the end of the afternoon had finished the bulk of the typing. Stretching her cramped limbs, she was just thinking of going for a quick cup of coffee when the door burst open and Kyle marched in.

Without a word, he flung himself down into a chair, his face shadowed and brooding, his mouth set into a hard line.

Every time Carrie was abruptly confronted with him like this, without time to get all her reactions under control, she was briefly flattened by the sheer physical presence of the man. His shirt, as usual, was open at the neck, revealing the gleaming, darkly tanned skin underneath; the long, powerful legs were encased in thin cotton jeans that did little to hide their supple outline; the black, shaggy hair dramatically emphasised the strong bones of that beautifully ugly face.

Seeing him in the flesh was very different from watching him on the television, she decided a little dazedly. When she'd seen him on the screen, her senses hadn't been assailed by the faintly musky scent of a healthy male body, she hadn't been able to see the pulse that beat rhythmically in the curve of his throat, feel the full force of those silver-grey eyes that could so easily turn stormy when he was aroused over something, as he clearly was now.

Nervously, she cleared her throat. 'Is—is something wrong?' she ventured.

'One of the pups has gone,' he stated flatly.

For a moment, she didn't have the slightest idea

what he was talking about. Then she remembered the wild dogs, the five little pups she'd watched playing around at the mouth of their den.

'Are you sure?' she asked, a lump swiftly forming in her throat.

'Of course I'm sure,' he growled irritably. 'I've been watching them all day. There's definitely only four left.'

Remembering their bright eyes, huge ears, skinny little white-tipped tails, she blinked hard a couple of times.

'Perhaps it's just got lost,' she suggested in a small voice.

Kyle turned the full brilliance of his gaze on her. 'Don't be naïve,' he told her roughly. 'It's dead. I suppose we're lucky that so far only one's been killed. It's not unusual for most of the litter to have disappeared by the time they're a few weeks old.'

'But that's dreadful,' she protested, hot tears beginning to sting her eyes. 'All those little puppies—something ought to be done——'

He swiftly got to his feet, gripping her shoulders, impatiently shook her.

'Grow up, Carrie! This isn't some nice, safe little safari park where there are keepers to look after the animals day and night. Out there,' he flung out one hand, pointed towards the plains that rolled into the distance, 'out there it's still savage and untamed. We're surrounded by hunters and predators, animals that have to prey on other animals in order to survive. If you can't accept that's the way things are out here, then get back to England where the only wild animals you'll see are in cages and have their meals brought to them twice a day on a tin plate. Only at least the animals here are free, they're not locked behind

bars and fences, forced to live unnatural lives so
that we can walk around pointing and gaping at
them.'

He let go of her as abruptly as he'd taken hold
of her, his eyes as fiercely bright as those of that
lioness she'd faced yesterday.

Oh wow, she thought shakily, it wasn't only
wild and savage outside the lodge. Every time Kyle
walked into a room he seemed to bring a great
draught of that primeval atmosphere right in with
him. On the surface, he could be all cool
sophistication and iron self-control, when he chose.
Yet underneath——

Her churning thoughts came to an abrupt halt
as he flung himself away from her and moodily
prowled across the room.

'Why on earth should you understand?' he
muttered broodingly. 'There's no point of contact
between your world and mine. We might as well
live on two different planets.'

Before she could say anything, he left the room,
banging the door noisily behind him. Feeling as if
she'd just been buffeted by a whirlwind, Carrie
collapsed into her chair, stared blindly out of the
window.

Too late, she was beginning to realise that he'd
been as upset by the death of that pup as she was,
that in an odd way he'd come here to share his
grief with her. And instead of giving him comfort,
she'd disappointed him by reacting childishly,
refusing to accept the harsh facts of life that
prevailed out here, where the whole ecological
balance revolved around the old maxim of the
survival of the strongest and fittest.

About to jump to her feet and run after him, to
explain that she *did* understand, even though she
found it hard to accept such a tough and merciless

way of life, instead she slumped back into her chair again. Surely he didn't really want her sympathy, her understanding? He was far too self-sufficient for that. The trouble was, she didn't really know what he did want from her.

Hard work, she decided at last, grimly turning back to the typewriter. After all, that was why she was here, wasn't it? To help him finish his book? Then that was exactly what he'd get from her, that and no more.

About to start pounding the keys again, she noticed a slim wallet lying by the table leg. She picked it up, then turned it over in her hands a couple of times. Was it Kyle's? She hadn't noticed him drop it. Of course, it could belong to Simon, or even Fergus. They'd both been in the office on previous days.

Slightly reluctantly, she opened it, thinking she might find some clue as to its owner. There was some money inside, a couple of credit cards—and tucked into a small compartment at the front, a small photo, just a head and shoulders snapshot of a very beautiful girl with a mass of long, blonde hair.

Carrie slid out the photo, then stared at it for a very long time. It was rather creased and slightly frayed around the edges, as if it had been carried around in this wallet for a very long time. A prized possession? A tiny chill settled in the pit of her stomach and steadfastly refused to go away.

Hurriedly shoving the photo back into the wallet, she was about to go looking for Kyle, to ask if the wallet belonged to him, when Simon poked his head round the door.

'Hi, sweetheart,' he said with a grin. 'Want to join me for a cup of coffee?'

'No, thanks.' She held out the wallet. 'I've just found this. It isn't yours, is it?'

He glanced at it, then shook his head.

'No, not mine. I think it might be Kyle's. Is there any identification inside?'

'There's a photo. I wasn't being nosy,' she added hastily, 'I just—well, I just happened to see it when I was looking for the name of the owner.'

'You should have tried looking at the credit cards. See? K. Allander. The wallet belongs to Kyle.'

She flushed slightly. 'I didn't think of that.'

He raised one eyebrow quizzically. 'I guess photos *are* more interesting than credit cards.'

'I wasn't prying!' she shot back instantly.

'Of course not. But now I'm as curious as you are. Who is this mystery girl being carried around in Kyle's wallet?'

He fished around, found the small snapshot, stared at it for a moment and then let out a long whistle.

'Well, who would have thought it?' he commented in a low tone. 'I always thought that was all over and forgotten a long time ago.'

The chill in Carrie's stomach seemed to spread.

'Who—who is she?' she asked, her voice slightly quavery.

'Estelle. His wife.'

'Wife?' It came out as a shrill squeak, and she quickly cleared her throat, tried again. 'I didn't even know he was married.'

'I should have said ex-wife,' Simon corrected himself. 'They were divorced several years ago. It was all very amicable, as I remember. Estelle had met someone else and Kyle agreed at once when she asked him for a divorce. I got the impression that he really didn't care too much, but it looks like that was just a front. No one carries a photo of his ex-wife around all these years unless there's a small spark of feeling still there somewhere.'

And knowing Kyle, it wouldn't be just a spark of feeling, Carrie decided miserably. He wasn't a man who did things on a small scale. With him it would be a grand passion or nothing at all.

It's nothing to do with you, she reminded herself vehemently. What he feels or doesn't feel—it's none of your business.

Pulling herself together, she took the wallet back from Simon. 'I'd better give this to Kyle. He might start worrying when he notices it's missing.'

She trailed rather reluctantly along to Kyle's room, tapped lightly on the door.

'Who is it?' came the slightly impatient query from inside.

'Carrie,' she answered nervously. 'I've—I've got your wallet.'

'Come on in.'

She pushed open the door, peered round it hesitantly, then bit her lip. Kyle was sprawled out on the bed, obviously snatching a quick nap, and he must have recently showered because he was wearing a short bathrobe which only just covered the essentials. Catching the flush of colour that instantly surged over her pale skin, he grinned wolfishly.

'Don't worry, I'm perfectly decent. At least, I am as long as I don't move too quickly.'

With exaggerated care, he sat up and swung his legs over the side of the bed. The robe flapped dangerously for a couple of seconds, but Carrie quickly averted her gaze and when she next looked at him, the robe was safely in place again. The trouble was, it didn't cover those long, tanned legs, the strong, well-formed feet, the powerful arms or most of his chest. All it did cover was—well, she really didn't want to think about that!

'If you're blushing, Carrie, it's because of what you're thinking and not what I'm actually showing,' he told her with mock sternness.

To her utter embarrassment, she blushed even more furiously, the colour sweeping over her in huge waves.

'You'd better explain what you're doing here before you burn up completely,' he prompted with some amusement.

'I told you, I found your wallet. I thought—I thought I'd better return it straight away, in case you wanted it.'

He turned his laconic gaze full on her. 'And what exactly would I use my credit cards for, out here?'

Drat the man, Carrie thought to herself vehemently. He somehow managed to make it sound as if she'd just been looking for some excuse to come to his room.

'All right, so I made a mistake,' she retorted irritably. 'You obviously don't care what happens to your wallet. Next time I find something of yours that you've lost, I'll shove it straight into the nearest cupboard and forget all about it.'

His hard mouth curved into an utterly disarming smile. 'I'm an ungrateful bastard, aren't I? You go to all this trouble to return my wallet and I can't even be bothered to say thank you. Why do you stay here, Carrie, and put up with my bad manners and my temper?'

'Haversham girls don't run away when the going gets a bit tough,' she muttered, rather thrown by his sudden change of mood.

'And has it been tough?' he prompted.

'Not exactly a bed of roses,' came her reluctant

admission. 'But don't worry,' she assured him, the light of battle gleaming in her eyes, 'I can cope.'

His gaze rested on her assessingly.

'Yes, I think that you can,' he mused at last. 'You look as fragile as a piece of porcelain, but I think you're really more like a solid iron pot, capable of standing up to endless wear and tear without too much damage.'

'Oh thanks,' she shot back sarcastically. 'That's just what every girl loves to hear, that she resembles an old iron pot!'

One black eyebrow lifted in amusement. 'Believe it or not, it was meant as a compliment. And no slur on your physical assets, of course. No man would dare denigrate them in any way, not without risking being called a liar.'

This conversation was suddenly becoming too personal, she decided with an acute twinge of unease. Especially as he was still sitting there wearing that disgracefully brief bathrobe. Time to bring it to a rapid halt.

'Well, I'd better be going——' she began, backing towards the door.

'Did I growl at you very much this afternoon?' he interrupted. 'I seem to remember I wasn't in a particularly good mood.'

Her face softened. 'That wasn't surprising, after finding out about the death of that pup.'

He gave a small shrug. 'I suppose I should be used to it by now, but I'm not. Every time an animal I've been watching gets killed or wounded, it hits me just as hard. Okay, so it was just one small pup, but I've been following its progress since the day it was born, watching it take its first steps, seeing it romping around with the others. And now it's gone, wiped off the face of the earth as if it never existed.'

His face had become taut, darkly shadowed, as if he held himself personally responsible for the death of that small pup. A little staggered by this unexpected streak of sensitivity, Carrie took an involuntary step forward, but then quickly checked herself. No matter how deeply that pup's death had affected him, he was quite capable of dealing with his own emotions, he didn't need a shoulder to cry on—and particularly not hers.

As if to prove her right, he lifted his head, quickly shook off his black mood.

'Perhaps we both need a little diversion to take our minds off things?' he suggested. 'I'm going out tonight. Do you want to come with me?'

'Going out?' she echoed, her mind briefly filled with thoughts of cinemas and theatres. Then common sense intervened. Civilisation of any kind was a couple of hundred miles away. Wherever he proposed going tonight, it certainly wasn't to see a film or a play!

'I'm going hunting with the wild dogs,' he told her. 'If you want to come along, be ready at sunset. I'm going to sleep for an hour now. Either leave or keep very, very quiet.'

'I'll leave,' she assured him hurriedly, but he didn't even seem to hear her. He'd already stretched out on the bed and closed his eyes, an utterly relaxed male, supremely confident in his own domain.

Fighting back a shameful urge to simply stand there and admire that sleekly powerful masculine body, Carrie instead turned round and fled from the room. Nor was she entirely sure if she was running away from him or from her own treacherously unreliable female instincts.

A sensible girl would have turned down his

invitation, she argued with herself weakly. A sensible girl would never have dreamt of setting out into the African night with a man like Kyle Allander. So why was she standing at the entrance to the lodge, waiting for him?

It was a question she didn't particularly want to answer, so she shoved it right to the back of her mind and then conveniently forgot all about it. In its place came a quiver of excitement. Night was falling fast, a huge full moon was already high in the sky, and there was the scent of something strangely primeval in the air. Her senses heightened, her skin prickling queerly, she stood there and breathed it in, felt it fizz round her system like champagne.

And yet underneath all the excitement, she was also paralysingly nervous. She was fifteen again, a girl on her first date. Uncertain, apprehensive, unsure of herself, all her limbs quivering slightly, like a young animal on the point of frantic flight away from something it didn't understand, had never experienced before.

'Ready?'

As Kyle's voice murmured in her ear, she jumped violently.

'Do you always creep up on people like that?' she demanded indignantly, her thundering pulses making her over-react.

He grinned. 'When you film animals, you get into the habit of moving around very quietly. No use barging in like an elephant, all you'll end up with is a shot of their backsides disappearing into the distance.' He glanced at the swiftly gathering darkness. 'Come on, time to get going.'

There's still time to change your mind, Carrie reminded herself as Kyle went on ahead of her. Yet her feet were already moving of their own accord, carrying her after him, and a couple of seconds later she shrugged and surrendered to the inevitable.

Once inside the Land Rover, Kyle turned to her.

'We've a bumpy ride ahead of us. Do that safety-belt up very tightly,' he instructed, 'and keep a close check on it. If it works loose, you could end up with a couple of broken bones.'

He started up the engine and the Land Rover moved off, yet he didn't switch on the headlights. The huge moon overhead gave off a pale silvery light that illuminated the plains and filled the potholes and gullies with contrasting black shadows, yet even so Carrie didn't know how Kyle could see where they were going. Miraculously, though, they didn't hit anything, didn't get the wheels stuck in any holes, even though the ride was every bit as bumpy as Kyle had promised.

'What did you mean earlier when you said we were going hunting?' she asked as they headed away from the lodge.

'Wild dogs nearly always hunt at night,' he told her. 'They cover miles, often travelling at fantastic speed. It's an incredible sight to see them loping across the plains.'

'Is that what we're going to do, then?' she queried. 'Park the Land Rover somewhere and watch them set off on their hunt?'

The moonlight briefly illuminated his face, revealing its strong pagan lines.

'Oh no,' he told her softly. 'We're going with them.'

Carrie gulped. 'Going with them? In the Land Rover?'

'That's right,' he agreed cheerfully. 'Of course, we might not be able to keep up with them right to the end, but we'll have a damn' good try.'

'You're mad,' she stated bluntly. 'Quite, quite

mad. No one goes hurtling round the plains at night in a Land Rover, not without getting killed. And for heaven's sake, put the headlights on! At least then we'll be able to see a few yards in front of us.'

'No headlights,' he said firmly. 'It'll distract the dogs. And stop clutching at my arm like that, I can't steer properly.'

Carrie hadn't even realised that her fingers were locked tightly around his forearm, digging deep into the hard muscles underneath. Hurriedly, she snatched her hand away.

'I still think you're mad,' she insisted.

'But it's a glorious kind of insanity, don't you think?' he challenged cheerfully. 'It's nights like this that let you know you're still alive.'

'No comment,' Carrie muttered darkly. 'We'll discuss it again when this is all over—if we're both still in one piece!'

Kyle was no longer listening, his attention was now fixed on something far ahead.

'There they are,' he told her quietly a moment later. 'Satan's pack, just setting off on their hunt.'

Peering out of the window, Carrie couldn't suppress a tiny thrill as she saw the dogs trotting along in single file, silhouetted against the darkening sky, nine—no, ten of them.

'Is that Satan in the lead?' she asked, her voice suddenly dropping to a whisper that could only just be heard over the sound of the engine.

'That old devil always has to be first in everything,' Kyle remarked drily.

'Like some people I know,' she muttered, flinging a meaningful look in his direction. He merely grinned. It was pretty obvious he wasn't going to let anything ruffle his high spirits tonight.

The pack was picking up speed now, and so was

the Land Rover. Despite the tight safety-belt,
Carrie was already being shaken from side to side
and she ruefully envisaged being covered with
bruises by morning. All the same, it *was* exciting,
hurtling through the night in hot pursuit of those
sleek dark shapes that were loping ahead of them,
the Land Rover often bucking violently yet
somehow miraculously missing the worst of the
pot-holes and rocks that littered its path.

Then the dogs were no longer in single file, some
of them began to swing out to the flanks. Carrie
squinted hard and suddenly caught sight of a dark
shape far ahead of them, the moonlight glinting on
the white patch on its rump—a gazelle! The dogs
were hunting a gazelle!

Stark reality hit her with a force that made her
gasp, shoving all the romantic notions right out of
her head. The heady excitement drained away in a
split second, in its place surged dark horror as she
realised exactly what was going to happen, what
she was about to witness. As all rational thought
fled, she flung herself at Kyle, frantically dragged
at his sleeve, his shoulder, anything she could get
hold of.

'No, don't let them, you've got to stop them!
Please Kyle, *do* something, oh you've got to *do*
something——'

Fighting grimly to keep control of the now
madly careering Land Rover, Kyle tried to free his
arm, needing both hands to steer the dangerously
swerving vehicle.

'Carrie, you're going to kill us!' he shouted
warningly.

'But those dogs—they're going to kill that
gazelle,' she yelled back with desperate urgency. It
was all she could think about, that one dreadful
thought pounded over and over inside her head,

driving out absolutely everything else.

The Land Rover slewed round, skidded and hit something hard, sending them both jolting forward with sickening force. Only their safety-belts saved them from serious injury. Then the engine cut out and suddenly there was deathly silence, a stark contrast to the noise and confusion of just seconds ago.

Kyle slumped back in his seat, released a shuddering lungful of air.

'I think,' he said in a voice vibrant with tension, 'that I might just strangle you for what you just did.'

And hearing his dangerously uncontrolled tone, Carrie began to tremble violently with reaction as she waited for his pent-up rage to break over her.

CHAPTER FIVE

To her surprise, he didn't speak again for a couple of minutes. Instead he drew several very deep breaths, as if deliberately trying to calm himself. Then, finally, he turned to face her.

She couldn't see his features clearly, only the pale glitter of those silver-grey eyes, and she began to tremble even harder.

'All right,' he said at last, his voice surprisingly calm now and more reasonable than she'd been expecting, 'let's talk this over. I'd really like to know why the hell you did your very best to smash us to pieces just then.'

With a feeble trace of defiance, she lifted her head. 'I can't stand blood sports!'

'Nor can I,' he agreed instantly. 'But what's that got to do with what happened tonight?'

She stared at him in disbelief. 'You saw what was happening as well as I did,' she accused. 'Those dogs were hunting that gazelle. If they'd caught it, they'd have—they'd have——' Her voice choked, trailed away.

'They'd have killed it and eaten it,' he finished for her quietly. 'That's not a blood sport, Carrie. It's how these animals live. They don't kill for fun, they kill because otherwise they'd starve. They're no different from any of the other animals around here that have to hunt in order to survive. The lions, the panthers, the leopards, the hyenas and jackals, and many more species, they're all predators. It's a simple fact of life—they hunt or they die.'

She remained silent.

'Another thing to remember is that they usually take only the sick or old animals,' he went on in that same steady voice. 'That helps to keep the herds healthy. And when they hunt, they often scatter the herds over wide areas. That helps to prevent in-breeding, which can be as bad for animals as it is for humans. And half the time, they don't even catch the animal they're chasing. That gazelle tonight had a fifty-fifty chance of survival, far better if it was in good condition.'

Carrie chewed her lip.

'I guess I behaved pretty stupidly,' came her subdued admission as Kyle's quiet voice calmed her, chasing away the white-hot chaos that had burned through her only minutes ago.

'My fault,' he apologised gently. 'I should have explained exactly what was going to happen, warned you that it was rather barbaric.'

'No,' she shook her head, 'not barbaric. Just nature in the raw.' She sighed softly. 'You're right, I was looking at it from entirely the wrong point of view. I wasn't thinking straight, I just reacted over-emotionally.'

'There's nothing wrong in not wanting to see an animal killed,' he told her a little roughly. 'Don't ever be ashamed of having the guts to stick up for what you think is right.' He groped under the dashboard and produced a torch. 'And now,' he added rather drily, 'I think I'd better take a look under the bonnet. Better start praying that there's no permanent damage. I don't particularly fancy having to walk all the way back to the lodge.'

Neither did she. There was something awesome, almost terrifying, about being out here on the plains at night, that vast moon glistening overhead, the eerie night sounds of Africa echoing all around them. Not wanting to stay in the Land Rover on her own, she quickly freed herself from the safety-belt and went to join Kyle.

'Hold the torch,' he instructed as she hovered nervously at his side. 'That'll leave both my hands free.'

He fiddled around under the bonnet for a while, then gave a small grunt.

'Everything seems okay. Luckily only the bodywork's smashed up, not the engine.'

Straightening up, he suddenly gripped her arm. 'What's that?' he demanded abruptly. 'Are you hurt?'

A little bewildered, she glanced down at the dark patch that stained the sleeve of her shirt; then she realised her skin was sore and throbbing in that spot.

'I must have knocked it,' she frowned. 'I don't think it's anything serious, though——'

Her voice trailed away and she gulped audibly as he reached into his jacket pocket, then brought out a small knife, the bright blade glinting wickedly in the silver moonlight. Instinctively she took a step backwards in alarm, but he hadn't relinquished his grip on her arm so she couldn't retreat any further. Then she gave a small yelp of sheer panic as he deftly ran the razor-sharp blade along the sleeve, slicing skilfully through the blood-stained material.

'I could have rolled up the sleeve,' she protested with nervous indignation as he parted the slit material, shone the torchlight on to the soft flesh underneath. 'Ouch!' she added with some feeling, as he prodded the broken skin. 'Stop doing that!'

He coolly ignored all her protests.

'Nothing too serious,' was his eventual verdict after carefully inspecting the small wound. 'Just a couple of surface scratches. I'll treat them as soon as we get back to the lodge.'

Her gaze locked with awed fascination on to the knife he still held in his hand.

'First a rifle, now a knife,' she muttered, half to herself. 'Why do I get the impression that you're a dangerous man, Kyle Allander?'

He lounged back against the side of the Land Rover, regarding her with eyes that had suddenly become brilliantly alert, yet as unreadable as any of the large cats that he so loved to film.

'Dangerous in what way?' he purred.

A deep unease began to steal over her, her legs were queerly shaky.

'I don't know,' she mumbled. 'It was a silly thing to say.'

He kept staring directly at her, causing a wave of heat to rush over her despite the chill of the night.

'You're wrapping your arms around yourself,' he observed softly. 'That's a self-protective gesture. Are you frightened of me, Carrie?'

'Frightened?' she blustered. 'Of course not. Anyway, what is this? Another lesson in body language? Well, thanks, but I'm not in the mood for lessons right now.'

'But I am,' he responded in that same low tone, his voice lapping over her like the touch of soft velvet. 'Quite suddenly, I'm very much in the mood.'

Too late, she realised that his fingers were still locked around her arm. Slowly, they closed more tightly around her bruised flesh; inexorably drew her towards him.

'God knows, I never intended this to happen,' he murmured. 'Perhaps I've just been shut away out here too long, not seeing a woman for weeks on end. And you are beautiful, Carrie. Do you know that? I'm not sure that you do. In fact, I don't think you know how dangerous you really are. Those huge blue eyes, so wide, so innocent—what do they hide? A tease or a true innocent? I just can't make my mind up about you. But there's one certain way to find out——'

As his voice thickened, alarm bells rang loudly inside her head. They were miles from anywhere, there was no one around to rush to her rescue if things got out of hand—and all her instincts were suddenly warning her that could so very easily happen. This was no callow boy who could be fobbed off with a few kisses, perhaps a couple of intimate caresses. Kyle Allander was a mature man, with all the deeply urgent wants and needs of the highly aroused male animal.

He'd drawn her so close to him now that she thought she could feel the radiant warmth from his body washing over her own. In just seconds, they'd be touching. Now was the moment to break away, tear herself from that iron grip, rush to the Land Rover and lock herself in.

She braced herself for the effort, yet never made it. At that instant, his thigh touched hers, causing her entire body to jolt in response to the electric contact. It sizzled through her, seared its way through every nerve-end, flooded her with bright, burning heat.

Humiliated by her body's weakness, she turned her head away. Immediately he gripped her chin, forced her to look at him.

'Don't be shy or ashamed,' he instructed. 'What's happening between us is no different from what's happening all around us a hundred, a thousand times out here on these plains tonight.'

'But—but that's different. They're wild animals!'

she flung back at him, her voice shrill with a mixture of fear and nerves.

'And so are we, deep down,' he told her calmly. 'Our basic instincts aren't so very different from theirs. Yet we've learnt how to hone them, refine them. We make love with care, with finesse, with special regard for our partner's pleasure.'

Her teeth were chattering now as her mind filled with vivid pictures of exactly how Kyle Allander would make love, with all the skill and finesse that his velvet voice had promised.

'Don't be scared, Carrie,' he soothed. 'There's nothing to be scared of, I promise you.'

'I'm n-not—n-not——'

The stammered words simply wouldn't come out, she couldn't bring herself to confess that she wasn't scared of him, but of herself. How many people would believe it? she wondered slightly desperately. She was well-travelled, highly qualified, so competent at her job—yet in other areas she was almost totally ignorant. Nothing quite like this had ever happened to her before. Oh, there'd been quite a lot of kisses, of course, some of them quite passionate, yet she'd always been content to go no further. There'd never been this dark, alien need that was now welling up from the secret places inside her. And he was hardly even touching her yet, just that gentle pressure of thigh against thigh. If he went any further——

A shudder rippled through her and she bit hard on her bottom lip. Was that what she was so afraid of? Of falling apart in this man's arms, a man who was adored by millions, who was only here with her tonight because there were no other attractive females within a hundred miles? Don't kid yourself, Carrie, she told herself slightly bitterly. If it were a straight choice between you and one of his sophisticated girlfriends, I'd bet a million pounds on the girlfriend every time.

He was studying her face carefully.

'You're fighting me,' he murmured at last. 'Inside that pretty little head of yours, you're fighting me. But your body's still talking to mine, Carrie. Why are you pretending you can't hear what it's saying?' His free hand slid round her back, gently coaxing her even nearer. Now they were lightly touching from head to toe, small points of contact shooting lethal sparks that threatened to ignite into a holocaust, given just the smallest of chances.

Through all the confusion came a tiny flutter of amazement. She'd never expected him to have so much patience, had been sure he was a man who simply took what he wanted, by force if necessary. But although she was his prisoner, trapped inside the circle of his arms, it was a gentle prison, she was sure she could break free if she could only find the strength. If he'd just stop talking, stop using that lethally charming voice to undermine all her defences, stop drowning her with the silent force of his personality, please let him just *stop*!

'You're still talking to me, Carrie,' came his caressing whisper in her ear. 'You're not saying a word, yet you're talking to me all the time.' He leant back against the Land Rover, drawing her with him so that she seemed to fit into all the hard curves of his body as her full weight sagged helplessly against him.

His fingers came up, lightly threaded their way through her hair, then slid down to the nape of her neck where they traced exotic patterns over her quivering skin.

'Do you know how much I want you?' he went on in a voice that was now slightly hoarse. 'Yes, of course you do, don't you?' And she did, his desire pulsed between them like a trapped bird, longing for the moment when it could fly free, soar up to the skies. How she longed to soar with it! Yet her feet were trapped on the ground, held fast by her own inexperience, her inhibitions, her cowardice.

Kyle's hand went on playing gently with the highly sensitive areas around her ears, the base of her throat, tiny thrills radiating out from his touch, gathering force, echoing through her entire body until she felt weak from their endless surging.

'Do you suppose it's the moonlight?' he muttered, the tip of his tongue following the path just traced by his shaking fingertips. 'They say the full moon makes all of us a little mad. And I certainly don't feel very sane tonight. Won't you kiss me, Carrie?' he groaned. 'Save me from this madness?'

Instinctively, she raised her head, caught a brief glimpse of those quicksilver eyes, gleaming fiercely now. This was a land of hunters, predators, she remembered with a small shudder. Then his mouth closed over hers, and all reasoned thought fled.

No longer gentle, his lips possessed hers with heated abandon, his tongue hungrily exploring, his hands leaving her hair, sliding down her flanks, holding her tight against him. Her own hands fluttered helplessly a couple of times, then crept round his neck, timidly exploring the powerful surge of muscles under supple skin, the silky texture of his thick black hair.

'We shouldn't do this,' she panted softly as he released her mouth for the briefest of instants, allowing sanity to momentarily return.

'Why not?' he growled, his fingers playing a

subtle rhythm against the back of her thighs,
causing small stomach spasms, sending all her
inner muscles into total disarray.

'Rule number one,' she gasped, frantically trying
to remember just what rule number one was, why
it was so important. 'H-Haversham girls must n-
never get involved with their clients.'

'To hell with the rules,' he ordered roughly.
'We'll obey them tomorrow. Say it after me,
Carrie. To hell with the rules.'

Her throat tightened as those dark features
loomed closer and closer, she could hardly get the
words out.

'To hell with the rules,' she whispered fearfully,
wondering what the consequences would be of this
abandonment of everything that had brought
order and harmony to her life.

He didn't even wait for her to finish. Already he
was feverishly unbuttoning her cotton shirt, the
breath was squeezed out of her lungs as those
clever fingers found the soft flesh underneath,
explored the rounded curves, lingered lovingly,
possessively on the hard tips.

'Body language,' he reminded her huskily.
'Speak to me, Carrie. But not with words.'

Uncertainly, her hands slid inside his jacket,
inside his shirt, slid over the supple skin, felt the
erotic sensation of the crisp hairs of his chest
brushing against her fingertips. New confidence
flared through her, followed by a deep need to
explore further this new world in which she was
treading, to learn more of its mysterious secrets.
Her fingers drifted down, found and followed the
narrow line of hair that arrowed down his
stomach, disappearing beneath the waist of his
jeans. His muscles contracted sharply under her
touch and an unexpected dart of triumph shot

through her as she realised how much power she had over him at this moment.

He muttered something under his breath, caught her tightly to him again so that she was starkly aware of the flare of his desire, his mounting tension as he fought to stop it tearing out of control. Then her body quivered helplessly as that dark head bent, raw hunger engulfed her as a lethal trail of kisses encircled her breast, moving steadily towards the throbbing peak, tongue subtly arousing, closing in, teasingly moving away again until her fingers moved convulsively in his hair, begging him for the touch that would——

'Oh,' she sighed raggedly as a sunburst of pleasure flattened her, but the small torment only led to a bigger torment lodged somewhere deep inside her, screaming for release, wanting, wanting—what?

He raised his head and the world briefly stopped whirling as her blurred eyes focused on him, saw the unleashed power, the burning need, the sheer maleness of him. Something inside her contracted, a small spark of fear leapt into life. She wasn't ready for this! A moment ago she'd been swept along on a river of pure sensuality but now, without any warning, she was desperately afraid of drowning, of being submerged by the sheer force of this man's personality, of somehow losing her own identity as his surging desire swallowed her up.

His hands were already on her stomach, gently circling, finding the catch on her jeans and undoing it, diving underneath into the warm darkness. As his unsteady breath fanned her cheek, she frantically tried to lose herself again in that winging pleasure, to ride on his touch, let go of reality. It just wouldn't work, though. The moment was past, her stomach was jumping now from nervousness, not desire, but how to tell him? He'd be angry, so very, very angry, he'd call her all the unpleasant names that men gave to women who led them on and on, only to pull away at the very last moment when it was almost too late for them to stop.

With a shiver of apprehension, she realised his hands had stopped moving, had drawn away from her clenched stomach muscles. Then they were drawing the zip of her jeans shut again.

So he knew! His head was turned away from her, not allowing her to see his face, but she could feel the shudders of frustration that rippled through him. She waited in terror for his scathing attack.

He dragged in a deep, unsteady breath, then another, finally ran his fingers through his hair as he released a ragged sigh.

'A lot of men would have wanted to kill you for what you just did,' he told her thickly. 'Or at the very least wouldn't have been willing to take no for an answer. You ought to say a small prayer of thanks that I've got more self-control than most.'

'I'm sorry,' she whispered inadequately. Instinctively, she reached out to touch him, to try and silently convey all the things that she just couldn't put into words.

A little savagely, he knocked her hand away.

'Don't push your luck,' he warned in a tight voice. 'I might have a lot of self-control, but I'm not superhuman. Go and sit in the Land Rover, leave me alone for a few minutes.'

Numbly, she obeyed him, curling up miserably in the seat and watching the dark shadow of his figure as he prowled around restlessly, his shoulders hunched moodily, his body tense.

It was quite some time before he returned to the Land Rover, flinging himself into the front seat beside her. That aura of tightly controlled need still emanated from him like an unseen cloud, filling the interior of the Land Rover with an atmosphere that hummed with potent emotion.

He stared out of the window for a couple of minutes, his fingers drumming lightly on the steering wheel. Then he turned to her, and she quivered under the force of that all-seeing gaze.

'So,' he said, his tone astonishingly soft, almost gentle, 'now we know.'

'Know?' she repeated nervously, unable to meet his eyes.

One strong finger lightly touched the side of her cheek, raising a storm of goose-pimples that raced all over her upper body. Then the pressure of that finger increased, forced her to turn and look at him, meet that silver gaze at full strength.

'Carrie the untouched, Carrie the unawakened,' he mused, almost in disbelief. 'That's it, isn't it? This is all new to you, you've never known what it's like to burn for someone's touch, nearly go out of your head wanting someone. So when it finally happened, it scared you half to death. How did it happen, Carrie?' he marvelled softly. 'How did someone like you reach the age of twenty-two without letting a man anywhere near you?'

Because I never met anyone like you before, she answered him silently. Because you're probably the one man on this earth who can make me feel the way I felt tonight. Then she quickly bit her tongue in case she blurted the words out loud. Kyle Allander didn't want to hear anything like that, she reminded herself a trifle bitterly. She'd already had that fact drummed into her. Sex without commitment, that was all he wanted. He wasn't interested in deep, long-term relationships, in fact he'd go out of his way to avoid them. Yes, he liked women—hadn't he proved that tonight?— but they had no permanent place in his life. And unless she wanted to end up emotionally bruised and battered, she'd better remember that.

He was looking at her intently now and frowning slightly. 'It's as well we found all this out in time,' he remarked, his voice much steadier now. 'Scared little virgins aren't quite in my line.'

Pride made her sit up straight, glare at him. 'Who said you were even going to have the chance of getting your hands on one?' she hissed, conveniently forgetting how she'd melted in his arms only minutes ago.

One black eyebrow lifted sardonically, but he didn't answer and somehow his silence was far more eloquent than any reply he could have made.

A dark flush stained her face.

'Kyle Allander, God's gift to women,' she muttered resentfully. 'Virgins throwing themselves at your feet, women fighting to scramble into your bed. Heavens, how on earth do you cope with the demand?' she went on with growing sarcasm. 'It must be utterly exhausting.'

'It is, but I do my best,' he answered lazily, a gleam now showing in his eyes. 'After all, I wouldn't want to disappoint any of them.'

The trouble was, the wretched man probably wasn't exaggerating, Carrie fumed to herself. She could so easily picture the long line of beautiful women who stretched back into his past, flitting in and out of his life as he drifted from casual affair to casual affair. She supposed she ought to be grateful that her face wasn't going to appear in the line-up, yet it was funny, all she could feel at the moment was a gnawing ache of regret.

'Come on, Carrie, use your brains,' he instructed as he watched the different expressions flickering revealingly across her face. 'There's no way it would ever work between us, even if there wasn't the big stumbling block of your virginity.'

'I've never heard anyone refer to it as a "stumbling block" before,' she informed him a little stiffly.

'It's how I regard it,' he stated firmly. 'I'm not going to go through the rest of my life feeling guilty because I snatched your innocence away from you. I can do without that sort of headache.'

'You didn't seem too worried about it earlier,' she reminded him, her cheeks burning again in the darkness as she unwillingly recalled that brief period of unrestrained passion.

'Moonlight madness,' he told her softly. 'It can afflict anyone on a night like this. But I'm over it now, and I'll make sure it doesn't hit me again.'

'I don't know why it ever happened in the first place,' came her subdued mutter. 'I thought blondes didn't turn you on.'

'Did I say that? Well, it's true,' he confirmed. 'Just look on tonight as a—temporary aberration.'

Ah, now she had him! A tiny spring of triumph welled up inside her.

'If blondes don't turn you on,' she goaded him rashly, 'why did you marry one?'

The fraught silence that followed was the most uncomfortable she'd ever experienced in her entire life. Why, on *why* hadn't she had the sense to keep her mouth shut? Too late, she realised how dangerous it was to bait this man.

The silver eyes were blazing ominously now. 'If there's one thing I can't stand,' he told her coldly, 'it's little snoops who can't keep their noses out of other people's private lives.'

Icy ripples slithered up and down her spine.

'I wasn't deliberately prying,' she mumbled, an apologetic note creeping into her voice. 'I saw that photo in your wallet, so I asked Simon who she was——' Her voice trailed away shakily, too late she realised that she'd now implicated someone else.

'In future, I'll warn Simon to keep his mouth shut,' he said tersely. 'Being on television doesn't make me public property, nor mean that everyone can go around discussing my private affairs behind my back.'

A last flicker of defiance sparkled in Carrie's eyes. 'But that's just the point, isn't it?' she pointed out recklessly. 'Your affairs *aren't* private, most of the time they're plastered all over the newspapers. Anyone can read all the sordid little details.'

He turned his head almost savagely and abruptly she shut up as she saw the look on his face.

'I've had about all I can take tonight,' he told her grimly. 'If you say one more word—just one——'

There was no need for him to finish his threat, the tone of his voice was enough to make her clamp her lips tightly shut, vow not to open her mouth again until she was a long, long way from him.

The engine roared into life, then he slammed it into gear, sending the Land Rover shooting forward. Carrie was jolted around until her teeth positively rattled, but she suffered it in stoic silence. In truth, she wasn't just physically shaken. Tonight she seemed to have run the entire gamut of emotions until now there wasn't anything left inside her except a painful emptiness.

With an enormous effort, she tried to sort out

her confused thoughts, work out just how she'd got
into this mess. For Kyle's part, the explanation
was perfectly simple. He was a very physical man,
she'd been aware of that from the beginning, and
it must have been weeks, even months, since he'd
touched a woman. Carrie wasn't so naïve that she
underestimated the strength of the male sexual
drive. Tonight, for some reason, it had reached
crisis point, and he'd blindly reached out for the
nearest female to hand—her.

So that neatly explained away Kyle's behaviour.
But what about her own? She hadn't exactly been
unwilling, at least not until the very end, when the
tumult of physical chaos had suddenly reached
fever pitch and scared her out of her wits. As it all
tumbled back into her mind, she felt peculiarly
hot, confused; her legs actually started to shake.

Moonlight madness—that had been Kyle's
justification for what had happened between them.
Yet surely she was too level-headed, too sensible
to believe in a myth like that? Glancing up at the
huge, glowing orb overhead, she gave a tiny shake
of her head. No, it just wasn't possible. That pale
light might bathe everything in an eerie silver
glow, but it couldn't make the blood pound
through your veins, rip away all your self-control,
send you tumbling headlong into the arms of the
very man you'd sworn to keep a safe distance
from.

Hero-worship then? Yes, that's what it had to
be, she decided with some relief. She'd worshipped
Kyle Allander from a distance for years, she'd
simply been overwhelmed at suddenly being with
him in the flesh, had given in to all those delicious
fantasies that had plagued her dreams since
adolescence. Only those dreams had abruptly
become reality as he'd started to undress her, and

that's when the fear had started. Because this wasn't the same man she'd adored from a safe distance, spellbound by the famous charm that radiated from the television screen. This was a flesh-and-blood human being, someone with an intriguingly quick and clever mind, a brief but fearsome temper, a lethal sexual attractiveness. No wonder she'd been bowled clean over—and frightened half to death.

Lights blazed out of the darkness, broke up the pattern of her wandering thoughts. They were back at the lodge.

'I suggest you go straight to your room, and stay there,' Kyle told her rather curtly.

Annoyed at his insinuation that she might have other plans—like trying to find her way to his room perhaps?—she was about to scramble out of the Land Rover and stalk haughtily into the lodge when she heard Kyle give an annoyed grunt.

What had she done *now* to annoy him? she wondered with some apprehension. Then she saw he was no longer looking at her, but at another Land Rover parked near to the front entrance to the lodge.

'Who the hell's that?' he growled.

'Perhaps a couple of tourists who've got lost and want to spend the night at the lodge?' she suggested helpfully. 'They do have safari tours in this area, don't they?'

'Not anywhere near this lodge. They always stick to the well-defined tourist trails,' came his slightly irritable response.

At that moment the door of the lodge opened and Carrie saw an older man with silvery hair silhouetted in the brightly lit doorway. Tall and distinguished-looking, he raised one hand in a salute as he saw their Land Rover.

'Sir Charles Kingwood,' Kyle told her, no longer sounding quite so annoyed.

'The name sounds familiar,' Carrie frowned, trying to remember where she'd heard it before.

'So it should. He owns a daily newspaper, several successful manufacturing concerns, a very large and impressive stately house in the Midlands—and he also happens to be my publisher.'

Carrie blinked.

'Do you mean he's flown all these thousands of miles just to check on how your book's coming along?' she asked in amazement.

'I'm several weeks behind schedule,' he admitted. 'Filming took longer than I expected, so the book had to take second place. And Sir Charles wants to get it out by the autumn, to catch the Christmas trade.'

Carrie could appreciate that. A new book by Kyle Allander always sold well, but sales would shoot up even further if it were published just before Christmas, when it would be snapped up by many people as an ideal present.

Kyle jumped out of the Land Rover, leaving her to scramble out and hurry after him as he walked over to the older man and shook his hand.

'I had a few days free, so I thought I'd fly out and see how you were getting on,' smiled Sir Charles.

'Don't you mean that you wanted to check on how the book was coming along?' prompted Kyle gently.

Sir Charles's smile broadened into a huge grin, then he actually chuckled. 'That's what I like about you, Kyle. You're so refreshingly straightforward. And how far *have* you got with the book?' he added slightly anxiously.

'It's almost half-finished.'

'Only half-finished?' repeated Sir Charles with obvious disappointment.

Kyle grinned. 'Don't worry, the last few chapters are already mapped out in rough draft, I can soon lick them into shape. And I've got a very efficient secretary who types them almost faster than I can write them. Carrie, where are you?'

She came forward into the light and gave Sir Charles a friendly smile, but was rather flummoxed by the startled expression that flashed across his face. Then she realised what she must look like, her clothes dishevelled, that blood stain on her shirt, her hair a tangled mess. Too late, she wished she'd had time to rush inside and tidy up before this introduction.

Sir Charles was still staring at her rather blankly.

'But where's Miss Jefferson?' he asked at last.

'Her mother was taken ill, she had to go back to England,' Kyle answered. 'Carrie—Miss Shepherd's from the same agency.'

'All the same, I wasn't expecting——' muttered Sir Charles, with a small frown. Then he seemed to remember his manners and held out his hand. 'Pleased to meet you, my dear.'

Carrie hastily rubbed her dusty hand on her jeans before returning the handshake.

'Sorry I look such a mess,' she apologised. 'We had—we had——'

She floundered slightly, wondering how she could explain away her appearance, in fact the entire events of tonight.

'We had a slight accident,' Kyle finished for her smoothly. 'Nothing serious, just a couple of dents in the Land Rover and a few bruises on us.'

'But what on earth were the two of you doing

out there on the plains at night?' exclaimed Sir
Charles. Then, seeming to realise exactly what he'd
just said, he hurriedly added, 'Not that it's any
business of mine, of course.'

Kyle stepped in with his usual cool composure.
'It was just a field trip,' he shrugged. 'Nothing of
any importance.'

Carrie was very sure those last words were
aimed directly at her, a warning statement. Don't
worry, she thought bitterly, I hear them, hear what
you're saying. All the same, she had to turn away
for a few seconds, away from that familiar, strong-
featured face, the eyes that saw too much, the
hands that knew exactly how to reduce her to
melting delight.

'Do you often go on field trips with Kyle?' Sir
Charles was asking her.

With a tremendous effort, she managed to drag
her attention back to the conversation.

'Sometimes,' she told him. 'Especially if he
wants me to take notes.'

'And were you taking notes tonight?' Sir Charles
persisted.

Carrie couldn't help thinking that he seemed
strangely disturbed about something, and she
wondered what it was.

'Tonight we were simply observing,' Kyle
answered for her. 'We were following a pack of
wild dogs as they set off on one of their hunts.'

Carrie remembered those dark shapes loping
across the plains, the wild beauty of the scene, the
silver gilding of the moonlight, and for a moment
a purely primitive response stirred inside her, like a
tiny flame licking at her insides. Caught unawares
by its insistent fierceness, she rather dazedly
stumbled after Kyle and Sir Charles as they made
their way into the lodge. I won't let this pagan

land get a hold on me, I won't! she determined a
little wildly as she followed them into the main
recreation room, where Simon and Fergus were
already waiting.

Starting to mutter some excuse about being
tired, wanting an early night, she fell silent as the
door opened behind her. Then her nose twitched
as a whiff of a very expensive perfume drifted into
the room.

The girl wearing the potent perfume appeared a
moment later, pausing briefly in the open
doorway—for maximum effect, Carrie couldn't
help thinking uncharitably—before strolling
slinkily into the centre of the room. Dark hair
framed a small, pointed, cat-like face with long,
slanting eyes that had been dramatically made-up
to emphasise their feline effect. Not exactly
beautiful, Carrie decided, but she certainly knew
how to make the best of what she'd got. And the
dress she was wearing was absolutely stunning, a
subtle, high-priced affair that clung sensually to
every curve and hollow and was nearly making
Simon's eyes pop out.

All the same, not exactly the kind of thing to
wear at a safari lodge, Carrie concluded. Not
unless you had some particular reason for wanting
to stand out like a diamond among a handful of
pebbles.

Sir Charles cleared his throat a little awkwardly.

'Er—I believe most of you know my daughter,
Lydia.'

The penny dropped. Lydia Kingwood! Now
Carrie remembered where she'd heard that name
before. Not because of Sir Charles, but through
his daughter, current darling of the gossip-
columnists. Lydia Kingwood, whose name had
been persistently linked with Kyle Allander's a few

months back—there had even been rumours of
wedding bells chiming in the future.

'I like tall, leggy brunettes,' Kyle had told her
once. And it was pretty clear now which tall, leggy
brunette he'd had in mind when he'd made that
statement.

Lydia swept further into the room, glanced
around.

'I think I know everyone here,' she purred
softly. 'Simon, how are you? And Fergus, nice to
see you again.'

Sir Charles looked slightly embarrassed. 'You've
overlooked someone, my dear. This is Carrie
Shepherd, Kyle's secretary.'

Those extraordinary eyes swept over Carrie
disparagingly, instantly taking in her crumpled
clothes, the bedraggled blonde hair, her pale, dirt-
smeared face.

'I'm afraid I never notice the hired help,' she
drawled. 'They just seem to fade into the
background, don't they?' Turning away from the
enraged Carrie, her eyes glowed even brighter as
they fixed on Kyle.

'Darling,' she breathed, 'I knew you'd be
missing me like crazy, so I persuaded Daddy to
bring me along on this little trip.'

And with that, she walked across the room,
entwined herself around Kyle and kissed him full
on the mouth.

Carrie couldn't stand any more. Feeling slightly
sick, she wheeled round to blunder out of the
room. She had a terrible feeling she was going to
cry and she wasn't going to do it here, in front of
all these people—in front of Lydia Kingwood.

She just made it to her room in time. Slamming
the door behind her, something dissolved inside
her and she flung herself on the bed, still fully

dressed, shut her burning eyes and held her hands to her aching head.

First, there had been that photo of Estelle, Kyle's ex-wife. Now Lydia Kingwood had turned up in the flesh. How many more women from Kyle's past were going to turn up to haunt her?

She closed her eyes even tighter to try and blot out their faces. This had been the weirdest, most disturbing night of her entire life. She'd never felt so utterly drained, so emotionally exhausted. And the worst part was, she didn't understand *why* she was feeling like this, *why* she was going through this nerve-wringing turmoil.

She was still trying to figure it out when the exhaustion finally caught up with her and completely swallowed her up. With a small whimper of relief, she slid down and down into a dark, dreamless sleep, finally finding a few hours of blessed peace.

CHAPTER SIX

A PERSISTENT noise seemed to be echoing inside her head. With a tiny groan, she forced one eye open, stretched her cramped body, which was stiff from lying curled up in a tight little ball all night.

The noise came again, resolved itself into an authoritative knocking at her bedroom door.

'Are you awake, Carrie?' demanded a familiar, imperious voice.

Carrie flinched. This was too much! Last night was still far too vivid in her memory, she simply wasn't ready to face Kyle again yet.

Hoping he'd go away if she ignored his loud knocking, she buried her face in the pillow, closing her eyes very tightly. Then she heard the door open, groaned inwardly as she realised she'd forgotten to lock it last night.

Although she stubbornly kept her eyes shut, she knew he was now approaching the bed. All her senses frantically registered his close presence, picking up those tiny invisible waves that radiated from him, warning her that he was no more than a couple of feet away.

'Good heavens, look at you!' came his slightly exasperated comment. 'You didn't even bother to get undressed last night.'

'I was tired,' she muttered defensively. 'I still am. Go away, I want to go back to sleep.'

'Not until I've attended to your arm.'

At that, her eyes finally flickered open. 'My arm?' she repeated, puzzled.

'I should have cleaned and dressed those cuts as

soon as we got back to the lodge last night,' he said a little testily, as if annoyed with himself for forgetting about it. 'But with Sir Charles' unexpected arrival, it went straight out of my head.'

'And Lydia's arrival,' she reminded him with a distinct trace of bitchiness. 'Don't forget the gorgeous Lydia.'

'No one forgets the gorgeous Lydia once they've met her,' he retaliated silkily, as if knowing perfectly well what lay behind her goading. 'At the moment, though, all I'm concerned about is your arm.'

'Well, you can just stop worrying, it's fine. Go and practice your first aid on someone else.'

Now that she was actually looking directly at him, she could see dark shadows of sleeplessness printed under his eyes, small, taut lines at the corners of that hard mouth. With some satisfaction, she decided that he'd had a thoroughly bad night. Then another possibility hit her, nearly knocked her flat, leaving her actually shaking with reaction. If he hadn't slept last night, there was one possible explanation that had absolutely nothing to do with insomnia. What if Lydia Kingwood were responsible for his present tired and drained state?

An unpleasant dizziness whirled inside her head, a painful ache gnawed at the pit of her stomach, then crawled along all her limbs. Yes, she decided unsteadily, that *had* to be the answer. Kyle had certainly been in a tense, frustrated mood after that disastrous encounter between them last night. How relieved he must have been when Lydia had so conveniently turned up. It was pretty obvious there was a close relationship between them— Carrie hadn't forgotten that intimate kiss Lydia had given Kyle last night—so there was no reason on earth why they shouldn't have simply picked up their affair again, two sophisticated, experienced people who knew exactly how to please each other.

Carrie's throat tightened, making it hard for her to swallow. No wonder Kyle looked tired. Lydia probably knew a hundred and one different ways of keeping a man awake all night!

And she didn't even know one, she thought dully, closing her eyes in humiliation. No wonder Kyle had found it so easy to control himself last night, to walk away from her when he'd discovered she was a virgin. A man like him wouldn't want to be bothered with silly little innocents. He was only interested in brief, uncomplicated affairs that could be painlessly ended when he was ready to start work on his next project.

'Carrie, have you gone back to sleep again?'

Kyle's voice pierced through her painful train of thought, and she winced at the underlying note of exasperation.

'No,' she answered in a low voice. 'No, I'm not asleep.'

'Then get yourself out of that bed and into the bathroom. Stay under the shower until you're spotlessly clean, then give me a shout and I'll come and put a dressing on your arm.'

'Why all this fuss about a couple of scratches?' she muttered, wishing he would simply go away and leave her to nurse this heavy ache grinding inside her.

'It's very easy for even a small cut to get infected out here,' he warned a little grimly. 'I don't want you to neglect those scratches and end up with blood poisoning.'

That made her slightly more willing to look at

things from his point of view. Dragging herself out of bed, she trailed along to the bathroom, where she stripped off her dusty clothes and stepped under the shower.

Remembering how important it was to use as little water as possible, she hurriedly soaped herself clean, rinsed off the lather, then wrapped herself in a huge, fluffy towel.

Peering in the mirror, she wrinkled her nose as she saw her wildly tangled blonde hair. Picking up a comb, she tried to tease out the knots, but a couple of them defeated her and she glared at her reflection, thoroughly fed up with the stubborn tangles. She should have had it cut before she'd come out here. It would have been much more practical to have had a shorter style. There just hadn't been time, though, for a visit to a hairdressers.

Rummaging around in the medicine cabinet, among the aspirins and other basic remedies, she found a small pair of scissors. Returning to the mirror, she grabbed hold of the knots in her hair, then impatiently snipped them off.

The trouble was, it looked rather lop-sided by the time she'd finished. She tried a few experimental snips in an effort to even it up, but somehow that didn't quite work either.

'Oh well, no point in doing things by half,' she decided philosophically, and set about systematically trimming the ends.

A quarter of an hour later, she was surrounded by a layer of chopped-off blonde curls and she was staring with open-eyed horror at the ragged-haired girl in the mirror.

'I don't think this was one of your better ideas, Carrie,' she muttered to herself. 'Didn't Mum always warn you not to do things on impulse?'

Quite suddenly, she absolutely longed to see her mother, talk to her, spill out all the things that had gone so drastically wrong since her arrival in Africa. But her parents were in South America; they wouldn't be back in England until the end of the year, when they were taking a brief holiday in London before setting off for the British Embassy in Paris, her father's next posting. She sighed softly. South America was such a very long way away. Although they kept in touch by phone and letter, it just wasn't the same as seeing them in person.

Yet perhaps it was just as well they were several thousand miles away at the moment, she decided with a grimace. She hated to think what they'd say if they could see her right this moment— particularly her mother, who'd always been so proud of her daughter's beautiful hair. Carrie took another appalled look at the scarecrow staring back at her from the mirror, then actually groaned out loud.

'Carrie? Are you all right?' a voice demanded sharply from outside.

Kyle! He must have heard that last groan. Panicking, she grabbed a towel, wrapped it around her shorn locks. Then she frantically tried to hide all the hair that littered the floor, pushing it under a small cupboard. She'd come back later and clear it up.

'I'm coming in,' Kyle called out decisively. A moment later, the door opened and he strode into the bathroom.

His black brows were drawn together, his face unexpectedly concerned.

'Did you hurt yourself?' he questioned. 'I thought I heard you call out.'

'I—er, I stubbed my toe,' she lied nervously.

That silver gaze flickered over her shrewdly, as if probing right inside her head. His only response was a non-committal grunt, though, and to her relief he didn't press it any further.

Opening the door of the medicine cabinet, he took out a bottle of antiseptic, a small dressing and a roll of bandage.

Carrie pulled the fluffy towel even more tightly around her.

'Perhaps I'd better get dressed first——' she began, a note of apprehension creeping into her voice.

'Don't be ridiculous,' he interrupted briskly. 'I'm going to bandage your arm, not try and seduce you.'

'Try and seduce me *again*,' she couldn't help muttering under her breath.

As his face darkened ominously, the muscles at the base of her neck tightened with tension.

'All right,' he frowned, 'do you want to talk about what happened last night, bring it right out into the open? Though I can't see what good it's going to do to go over it all again. It happened, it was a mistake, and it'll make life a lot easier for both of us if we just forget all about it.'

Easy for him to say that, she thought resentfully, watching him with strained eyes as he deftly measured out a length of bandage. To him I'm just one more pretty face in a long, long line of pretty faces. He'll forget I ever existed the moment I leave here. But to me, he's——

The room seemed to become very still, she stopped breathing, even her heart seemed to stop beating. Then alarm thundered through her as the truth burst inside her head.

'He's beginning to become the centre of my entire world.'

She was so stunned that she nearly said it out loud. Ohh God, she *hadn't* actually said it, had she? Frantically, she tried to remember. No, it was all right. That burst of revelation was still safely hidden inside her head, he hadn't heard it, would never hear it.

Too late, she remembered his clear instructions on her arrival here. No starry-eyed hero-worship, he'd told her. Only this wasn't a schoolgirl crush, she knew that now. Well, she'd just have to be very, very careful in the future, make sure he never found out that his silly little secretary had fallen for the one man on earth that she couldn't have.

Kyle was talking again now, his distinctive voice slowly breaking through the numb sense of shock, his words only gradually beginning to make sense.

'Do you really want an explanation for what happened last night? It's perfectly simple, Carrie. The African night, the bright moonlight, the excitement of that chase across the plains—they all forced you into a certain frame of mood, a state of excitement. I responded to that excitement, and after that we just sparked each other off.'

'So it was all my fault?' she accused, angry that he should be trying to shift all the blame on to her shoulders, but at the same time terrified that she'd say something, do something that would give her away.

'In a way,' he agreed calmly. 'You wanted me. Don't try to deny it,' he warned as he saw an explosive protest gathering inside her. 'For a while there, before you got scared at the way things were going, you really wanted me. That's why I found it so hard to stop, to pull back. Being wanted by someone is the biggest turn-on in the world. Don't you know that?'

Quite suddenly, she didn't want to argue with him any more.

'Just bandage my arm, will you?' she asked tiredly. 'I'm—I'm getting cold, I want to get dressed.'

It only took him a minute, but it seemed the longest minute of her entire life. She never even felt the sharp sting of the antiseptic, only the light, sure touch of his fingers as they cleaned the scratches, applied the small dressing, secured it in place with the expertly tied bandage.

'There,' he said finally with a grin, as if addressing a small child. 'All better now?'

'Yes, thanks,' she answered, then with a feeble attempt at light-heartedness, added, 'Do I get a lollipop for being a good girl?'

'No, just a kiss,' he told her promptly, and before she could protest or her muscles had time to tighten with apprehension, he leant over, lightly kissed her forehead.

'You see?' he teased. 'No sparks this morning. Everything's back to normal again.'

Except that her skin seemed to be burning where his lips had touched it. And wasn't he spending just a little too much time clearing away the bandages and antiseptic, not letting her see his face for a couple of minutes?

Stop kidding yourself, she scoffed. That kiss had meant no more to him than a sneeze!

She jumped up, suddenly needing to get away from him before she did or said something very stupid.

To her relief, he didn't try to stop her leaving. Fleeing back to the safety of her bedroom, she locked the door, then with quivering hands unwrapped the towel from her head, stared with shocked eyes at her devastated hair.

Had she done it on purpose? she wondered a little wildly. A sort of self-punishment for what had happened last night? She didn't know, couldn't trust her own judgment any more.

One thing was certain. Kyle Allander wouldn't look twice at her any more, not now she looked such a freak. Lydia Kingwood would have a clear field from now on.

He likes wild cats, she thought to herself with uncharacteristic bitchiness. Well, now he's got one because Lydia's a cat if ever I saw one! And I hope she scratches him where it really hurts!

Then her brief spurt of defiance petered out and, sinking down into a small huddle on the floor, she rather drearily began to cry.

It seemed ages before those humiliating tears finally stopped spurting out. Head aching, eyes throbbing, she slowly dressed, then tried to repair her ravaged face with skilfully applied make-up. Several minutes of fiddling with a comb made absolutely no difference to her ragged hair, so in the end she simply gave up and left it as it was.

Although she'd have liked to have been a complete coward and stayed hidden away in her room all day, there was work to be done—a couple of revised chapters waiting to be typed. Desperately hoping that she wouldn't bump into anyone, she scurried along to her office, then quickly closed the door behind her. So far, so good. Now, if she could just avoid everyone for the rest of the morning . . .

A fresh pile of paper on her desk caught her attention. Picking up the top sheet, she glanced at the familiar, almost indecipherable scrawl, then gave a small frown. This hadn't been here yesterday, it was a fresh chapter, which meant . . .

Her heart seemed to turn a somersault, leaving her giddy and breathless. Which meant that Kyle must have been working on it for most of last night! No bedtime games with Lydia Kingwood after all.

That wasn't to say that he wouldn't leap straight into Lydia's bed tonight, she warned herself. But right at this moment that somehow didn't seem to matter. The black clouds scudded away and she hummed cheerfully to herself as she inserted a sheet of paper into the typewriter, then began thumping away at the keys.

A few minutes later, the door opened and Simon poked his head round.

'Do you think you could type a letter for me, Carrie——' he began, then his voice petered out and he stared at her in wide-eyed disbelief.

'Don't say anything!' she ordered. 'I *know* what it looks like.'

He came further into the room to gaze sorrowfully at the ragged ends.

'But why did you do it?' he lamented. 'Your beautiful hair!'

'I decided to give it a trim,' she shrugged. 'The only trouble was, I got rather carried away and cut off more than I meant to.'

'And with a blunt pair of scissors, by the look of it,' commented Simon, studying it gloomily. 'It's a total disaster.'

'Thanks for those few comforting words!'

'Sorry,' he apologised, 'I didn't mean to be quite so brutally blunt. It's come as rather a shock, though. You see, Fergus and I were rather relying on you.'

She stared at him warily. 'To do what?'

'To—er—to try and stop Kyle getting involved wth Lydia Kingwood,' he confessed rather sheepishly.

Carrie somehow fought back the colour that threatened to creep into her face, cleared her dry throat before finally speaking again.

'Would you like to explain that a little further?' she said carefully.

Simon pulled up a chair and sat down opposite her, his face unexpectedly earnest.

'Neither Fergus nor I can stand Lydia,' he confided. 'She might be gorgeous in a slinky kind of way, but she's also a complete bitch. Kyle escaped from her clutches once before—went off to the Galapagos Islands to do some research for an article on giant tortoises—but someone like Lydia doesn't give up that easily. And now she's followed him out here.'

'Sir Charles wanted to find out how Kyle's book was coming along,' Carrie pointed out. 'I suppose it was only natural Lydia should come with him.'

'Rubbish!' snorted Simon. 'If Sir Charles had wanted to know about Kyle's book, he could have written him a letter. We're not entirely cut off from the rest of the world, you know, we collect the post twice a week when we fetch our supplies. No, the idea was Lydia's, you can bet on that. She's going to try and catch Kyle by planting herself under his nose all the time and simply wearing him down.'

'I don't think Kyle's the type who wears down easily,' Carrie commented with some acerbity.

Simon merely looked gloomy. 'Maybe not. But if something's flashed under your nose for long enough, in the end you usually grab it, even if you don't really want it. And Lydia's got a lot of cute little tricks up her sleeve. Even Kyle might not be immune to all of them.'

'So you and Fergus decided to recruit me to

distract Kyle from the luscious Lydia?' she accused
in disbelief.

'It did cross our minds,' he admitted. 'Nothing
too serious, of course, we weren't expecting you to
jump into bed with him or anything, just—well—
distract him——'

'Flash my legs around?' she suggested sarcastically. 'Leave the top buttons of my shirt undone,
something like that?'

To her amazement, Simon nodded eagerly.
'That's it exactly.' Then his face dropped. 'Only
now you've made such a mess of your hair, I can't
see it working,' he added gloomily.

'Simon,' she said gently, 'I'm very tempted to
drop this heavy typewriter right on to your thick
head from a great height.'

His brown eyes looked mournful. 'It wasn't a
good idea?'

'You've got it in one. Not a good idea at all,'
she told him in a flat voice.

He gave a resigned shrug. 'It was worth a try.
Sorry if I upset you, Carrie. I was only thinking of
Kyle.'

'It seems to me that everyone thinks far too
much of Kyle,' she retorted crisply. Including me,
she added silently with a small sigh. 'Let him fight
his own battles,' she added. 'I'm sure he's more
than capable.'

'You're probably right.' Simon got up, ambled
over to the door, then paused. 'Why don't you go
and see Fergus about your hair?' he suggested.
'When we're away on location, he cuts the hair of
all the film crew. Does quite a good job of it, as
well.'

'That's just what I need,' she commented a little
exasperatedly, 'a short back and sides.'

'It can't look much worse than it does now,' he

told her with a cheerful lack of regard for her
feelings. 'Take my advice, Carrie, go and see
Fergus.'

After he'd left, she fingered the uneven ends of
her hair, then sighed despondently. Could Fergus
leave it looking any worse than it did already?
Probably not, and at least he might be able to
neaten it up a little.

Abandoning her typewriter, she went off in
search of Fergus. Remembering that he often sat
out on the verandah while he prepared the
vegetables for the evening meal, she pushed open
the outer door and was momentarily blinded by
the blazing sunshine. Her eyes soon adjusted to the
bright light, then she groaned under her breath as
her gaze fixed on the sleek body stretched out on a
towel, sunbathing.

'Heavens, it's the little secretary,' drawled Lydia
in a bored voice. 'Aren't you meant to be working,
sweetie? I'm sure Kyle doesn't pay you to wander
around all day doing nothing.' Then those cat-like
eyes opened in transparent delight as she noticed
Carrie's cropped hair. 'Good heavens,' she
breathed, 'you look an absolute sight.'

The last of Carrie's self-esteem fled. Turning
round, she bolted back into the lodge, so close to
tears that she didn't even see Fergus until she
cannoned straight into him.

Somehow Fergus made sense of her garbled plea
for help. Sitting her down in a chair, he patted her
shoulder comfortingly.

'I'll just go and fetch some scissors. I won't be long.'

He was back in a couple of minutes with comb
and scissors. After wrapping a towel around her
shoulders, he then ran the comb through her
massacred hair a few times, as if trying to work
out just what could be salvaged from the mess.

'Right, let's see what we can do,' he grunted finally, and had just picked up the scissors when the door opened and Kyle walked in.

Carrie's spirits instantly plummeted to new depths. The one person on this earth she didn't want to see right now, not while she looked such a fright!

'I thought I ought to let you know, Fergus, that Sir Charles and I won't be here for lunch,' Kyle said casually. Then his silver gaze drifted over to Carrie. 'Having your hair trimmed?' he remarked. 'Good idea, much more practical in this heat.' Then he strolled out again.

As the door closed behind him, Carrie gaped in astonishment. 'He didn't even *notice* that I'd chopped it to bits and ruined it,' she marvelled. 'Everyone else took one look and said how awful it looked. He didn't even seem to see it.'

Fergus merely grinned. 'Ever heard the old cliché about love being blind?' he suggested slyly.

'Fergus, don't tease me, not right now,' she begged, trying to ignore the slamming beat of her heart at his flippant suggestion.

Twenty minutes later, Fergus finally put down his scissors. 'I've done my best,' he told her. 'Wash it, then let it dry naturally. I think you'll be surprised at the result.'

'I was surprised after I'd finished cutting it,' she commented glumly. 'I think I can do without another surprise like that one.'

All the same, she faithfully followed his instructions, and in an hour's time was staring at her reflection in sheer amazement.

Fergus had worked a major miracle. Her head was covered with a halo of softly curling glossy hair, the skilfully cut lines subtly emphasising the long, slim line of her neck, the delicate curve of her cheekbones, her huge, long-lashed eyes.

'Wow!' she breathed, a little awed. 'I should have left Fergus a huge tip.'

Head held high, she pranced confidently into lunch and was most gratified by the glowering look on Lydia's face as she saw Carrie's gleaming head of hair and heard the compliments that Simon and Fergus showered on her.

For the rest of that day, she slaved away at the typewriter, working on the pages of scrawled notes that Kyle had left from last night. Fortunately, she rarely tired of typing his material; it was never the dull chore that it could so easily have been. His style of writing reflected the man himself, intelligent, fast-moving, utterly absorbing, so that she found herself typing faster and faster as she was swept along by the sheer pace of the narrative.

She didn't particularly enjoy dinner that evening. Lydia had grabbed the seat next to Kyle and the food stuck uncomfortably in Carrie's throat as she had to sit and watch the other girl constantly touching Kyle's hand, his arm, in fact almost every part of his anatomy she could decently touch in public. As soon as she'd forced down the last mouthful of food, Carrie hurriedly excused herself and fled back to the study. For another couple of hours she pounded out her frustration on the typewriter; then she pushed the sheets of typing to one side, flung herself out of her chair and prowled restlessly over to the window.

Fresh air, that was what she needed. She'd been cooped up in this little room all day, it was beginning to seem like a prison. No chance of a walk, of course. That horrifying encounter with the lioness was still crystal-clear in her memory, she had no intention of ever setting foot outside the lodge unless someone was with her. She could sit out on the verandah, though, enjoy a few minutes of peace as dusk softly fell.

She let herself out through one of the side doors and thought for a few moments that the verandah was deserted. Then a tiny groan sounded in her throat as she saw the dark figure sprawled in a chair at the far end.

Kyle Allander, the very last person she wanted to see right now.

About to retreat hastily back into the lodge, she instead quivered uncertainly as he raised his head at that instant and fixed that penetrating gaze directly on her. It nailed her to the spot; drained all the strength from her legs.

'There's no need to run away,' he told her. 'Come and sit with me for a while.'

Why did his invitations always sound more like orders? she wondered a little desperately. But her shaky legs were already carrying her towards him, and a few seconds later she collapsed into the chair by his side.

He didn't say another word and his silence slightly unnerved her. Then she realised he was staring at something in his hand. Her gaze followed his and her nerve-ends abruptly caught fire as she realised exactly what he was staring at.

It was the snapshot of Estelle, his ex-wife. How often did he sit here like this? she wondered dully. Staring at that photo and wishing that he had his beautiful wife back again?

She cleared her dry throat and prayed hard that her voice would sound fairly normal when she spoke.

'Is—is that the only photo you have of your wife?'

'She's not my wife,' he corrected her, slightly harshly. 'Not any more.'

'I'm sorry,' she whispered, clutching her shaking

hands hard together in an effort to stop their betraying movement.

The black head came up sharply, the silver gaze raked over her.

'Sorry?' he repeated with a frown. 'About what?'

She made a small, helpless gesture. 'Well—that your marriage didn't work out,' she somehow managed to get out in a cracked tone.

His frown deepened, the black brows drawing together in a brooding expression. 'It was all my fault. I should never have married her.'

This time, Carrie remained absolutely silent, not trusting herself to speak.

Kyle studied her pale face, then gave a tiny growl deep in his throat.

'What's going on inside that funny little head of yours? Do you think I regret the divorce? That I'm still in love with her?'

At that, her eyes flew open very wide. 'A-aren't you?' she stammered in a tiny little voice.

'I'm not sure that I ever *did* love her,' he muttered, almost as if talking to himself. 'Oh, Estelle was gorgeous and I was certainly infatuated, but love? I'm not sure I even knew the meaning of the word. Perhaps I don't even now. My parents had just died though, a bloody stupid car crash on the motorway that wiped both of them out in a couple of seconds, and suddenly I was all alone in the world. I guess I needed someone very badly at that time and then, out of the blue, along came Estelle. She was the loveliest girl I'd ever seen, with the kind of body that would make most men commit murder to spend just one night with her. I was young, inexperienced—oh yes, even I was inexperienced once,' he added wryly, seeing the disbelieving look on her face, 'although I've certainly made up for it since. Anyway, I completely lost my head. I proposed to Estelle only a couple of weeks after I'd met her and we were married a few days later.'

'But you must have loved her a little,' insisted Carrie, trying hard to keep any note of jealousy out of her voice.

'I certainly wanted her,' Kyle admitted with rough honesty. 'Is that the same thing? Some people would think so—although I don't somehow think you're one of them. We were good in bed, but that wasn't enough to hold us together in the end. It never is, no matter how important physical attraction might be at the beginning of any relationship.'

Carrie tore her gaze away from him to stare out into the gathering darkness.

'What happened?' she questioned softly.

He didn't answer immediately. Then, just as she thought he wasn't going to tell her any more, that taut voice started speaking again, as if he badly needed to make a full confession.

'I was just starting out on my career. I'd already made one documentary and was working very hard on a couple of others. Unfortunately, it meant I was away from home a great deal, and Estelle simply couldn't take that. She looked like a top model, she had sex-appeal dripping out of every pore, but it was all a front, at heart she was just a home-girl. She could have made the front page of all the glossies if she'd wanted a modelling career, but all she longed for was a nice home, a couple of babies and a husband who worked nine to five and was home every evening and weekend.'

Her eyes sparked with a first glint of indignation. 'And you wouldn't give up your career for her?' she accused, her voice hardening slightly.

'Not wouldn't—couldn't,' he answered simply.

'It's in my blood, it's what I was born to do. I tried not to take on any assignments abroad when I realised things were going badly wrong, made an effort to get home more often, but by then it was already too late. Estelle had met someone else, someone who could give her the stable home life she craved. Since it was obvious she was genuinely in love with this man, I didn't stand in her way when she told me she wanted a divorce.'

'You make it sound so—oh, I don't know,' she said with a small shudder. 'So cold, so unfeeling, as if none of it touched you at all.'

He shook his head slowly. 'Not true. It knocked my confidence to·hell and back. The divorce might have been what they laughingly call friendly, there were no terrible rows and, thank God, no kids to suffer because of the break-up, but for months, even years, I felt like a complete failure. I think that anyone whose marriage has broken up goes through that. It's a lousy feeling, you lie awake at night going over and over it inside your head, trying to work out where you went wrong, what you could have done to make the marriage work. Stupid and futile when the whole thing's finished, but there's no way to stop it happening. You just have to somehow drag yourself through it, keep working harder and harder so you don't have too much free time to sit and constantly brood about it.'

His confession shattered her. Kyle Allander admitting to weakness, human failings, black depression—it was as unbelievable as someone telling her that the moon really was made of cheese.

'Why are you telling me all this?' she asked very shakily.

He stared blankly ahead of him for a couple of

minutes, then finally gave a strangely indecisive shrug.

'Why?' he repeated in a low monotone. 'I don't know. Do I have to have a reason?' He paused, then added almost absently, 'There's only one I can think of. "The night is dark and I am far from home." Will that do?'

'Is that a quotation?'

He shrugged again. 'I think it must be. Something I once read, something I once heard—does it matter?'

He was right, it didn't matter. The words echoed softly round and round inside her head. 'The night is dark'—yes, she could feel the darkness closing in around her, isolating her, letting her briefly share his self-imposed loneliness.

She glanced at him, saw his face was strangely drawn as his hands turned that small photo over and over, as if it were a magic charm that could somehow put everything right, make the past disappear.

Then, to her shock, he abruptly tore the photo into two, then four, tossed the pieces over the edge of the verandah.

'You shouldn't have done that!' she exclaimed swiftly, jumping to her feet. 'I'll find the pieces for you, stick them together again——'

He swung himself out of the chair, came to stand just behind her.

'No, leave it,' he ordered roughly. 'There's only one reason why I've been carrying that photo around for all these years. It was a reminder to myself not to make the same stupid mistake all over again. A job like mine doesn't allow for any permanent relationships. I learnt that the hard way and it's a lesson I shan't ever forget, I don't need that photo to keep rubbing it in.'

Her fingers curled tightly around the rail at the edge of the verandah. 'Yet there must be times when you want——' Her voice trailed away unsteadily as she felt the warmth of his breath lightly drifting over her bare neck.

'When I want?' he prompted gently, his tone suddenly very different, a little husky, as if his throat were as dry as her own.

She couldn't answer him. He was still standing behind her, only a couple of inches away now, that hard body so tantalisingly close, all she had to do was lean back slightly and they'd be touching, touching——

'When I want something like this?' he murmured, his hands coming round her, drifting across her flat stomach, slowly, gently rising, brushing the underswell of her breasts, pausing there to lovingly support their fullness. 'I like you with your hair shorter,' he breathed softly. 'It leaves your neck beautifully bare.' His lips touched the vulnerable spots, making her shudder violently. Then his tongue gently traced the delicate line of her spine as it disappeared under her jumper, closely followed by a series of meltingly sensual kisses that brought fire to her skin, made her eyes droop heavily as a languid response stirred deep inside her.

For an instant he buried his face in her short, silken hair, his hands digging almost convulsively into the softness of her breasts as if imprinting the feel of them on to his palms, to be savoured over and over later, when they were apart. Then the breath shuddered in his lungs, he seemed to make a tremendous effort to get control of himself again, and, abruptly he let go of her.

'Ah, Carrie, I think you could drive me totally out of my mind, if I let you,' he murmured hoarsely. 'But I'm not going to let it happen, I'm *not*. I'd be mad to give in, put us both through that sort of hell. I couldn't face it again, and as for you, you're not like Estelle, you wouldn't be able to find someone else when we broke up. You're a one-man girl, I can see it in those beautiful sapphire eyes of yours.'

Wanting him to touch her again so badly that it was a gnawing ache deep inside her, she clenched her small fists, dug her nails cruelly into her palms to stop herself going on her knees in front of him, begging him to give them both a chance.

'You've no idea what I'm really like, what I'm capable of coping with,' she whispered.

Although she wasn't looking at him, was frightened to face him in case she broke down completely under the blazing gaze of those desire-filled, silver-grey eyes, she knew that he was now shaking that dark head of his decisively.

'It wouldn't work, not with the kind of life I lead. I've already proved that. And I swore that I'd never again make promises that I simply can't keep.' His lips touched the nape of her neck for one last time, as if he very badly needed a lingering reminder of the sweetness of her skin. 'Find someone else,' he instructed huskily. 'You need a man in your life, Carrie. But it won't—it can't—be me.'

CHAPTER SEVEN

DAMN Estelle! thought Carrie in utter misery as she tossed her way restlessly through the long, long night that followed. Because of her, Kyle was convinced that no woman could cope with his nomadic, unsettled lifestyle. It was an irrational attitude, perhaps, but the trauma of his divorce had obviously left deep scars and she instinctively knew that it would be useless to try and persuade him that he was wrong. At last, she was beginning to understand this enigmatic man. There was a mental block in his mind about this, and there was absolutely no way that she would ever be able to get round it.

Getting up heavy-eyed the next morning, she was very relieved when Kyle didn't put in an appearance at breakfast. Not that it really made any difference to her appetite, she still couldn't force down a single mouthful of food. After choking her way through half a cup of coffee, she hurriedly retreated to the tranquillity of her office.

Winding a sheet of paper into the typewriter, she tried hard to lose herself in her work, not to let her thoughts go wandering down dangerous paths that led to all sorts of pain, but it was useless. Nothing would blot out the memory of last night.

She knew Kyle must have worked very late after he'd left her because the chapters she'd typed yesterday had been radically altered and revised. Whole paragraphs had been scored out with forceful black lines, as if the writer had taken out his frustration on the pen, and the distinctive ting was even more indecipherable than usual. Sorting it all out, trying to make sure that the new insertions went in the right places, eventually gave her a thundering headache. About to take a break and go in search of some badly needed aspirins, she gave a small grimace as there was a light tap on the door.

A moment later, it opened and Sir Charles walked in.

'I do hope I'm not interrupting your work,' he said in his distinctive voice. 'I was hoping we could have a talk about something—well, fairly personal.'

'I'm rather busy——' Carrie began tiredly.

'Of course you are,' he agreed smoothly, coming further into the room, 'and I do apologise for disturbing you, but I really would like a private talk with you.'

With a bleak sigh of resignation, Carrie pushed her typing to one side, swung round to face him.

'What's this all about?' she asked without much interest.

Sir Charles looked uncharacteristically embarrassed. He shuffled his feet a couple of times, then nervously cleared his throat. 'Actually, it concerns—well, in a roundabout way it concerns my daughter, Lydia.' He looked even more awkward, wiped his damp forehead with a gleaming white handkerchief, and seemed to be wishing he were a million miles away.

'Why not just say exactly what's on your mind?' Carrie suggested.

'All right,' he agreed with some relief. 'I'll be absolutely blunt. I want you to leave here and go back to England.'

For a moment she stared at him in utter astonishment. Whatever she'd been expecting, it certainly hadn't been this. Then everything suddenly clicked into place and she fought back a sudden spurt of anger.

'So Lydia can't stand competition of any kind. That's it, isn't it?' she challenged in some disgust. 'If I were twenty years older or plain as a pikestaff, we wouldn't be having this conversation, would we?'

Sir Charles had the grace to look momentarily discomfited. Then he gave a brief shrug. 'To be perfectly frank, no we wouldn't. But you're not plain, my dear, quite the reverse in fact, so I'm here to try and resolve the situation.'

Her blue eyes flared mutinously. 'As far as I'm concerned, there isn't any "situation",' she answered tightly. 'I work for Mr Allander and that's as far as it goes.' Stubbornly, she pushed away memories of last night, the soft, lethal touch of Kyle's lips against her neck. Her mouth took on a new, hard line. Any relationship between them was definitely out. Kyle had told her that himself with stark bluntness and he'd meant it. She wasn't actually lying to Sir Charles, just not telling him the entire heartbreaking truth.

Sir Charles smiled at her rather distantly. 'If you're just his temporary secretary, it really won't make any difference to you if you return to England, will it?'

Oh clever, very clever, she conceded bitterly. He'd taken her own words and used them against her. A little panic-stricken, she realised she was fast running out of excuses to stay here at the lodge.

'I don't like to leave a job half-finished,' she protested. 'There's still a lot of work to be done on Kyle's book.'

'No problem,' he assured her smoothly. 'I know

Miss Haversham very well, I'll get in touch immediately and ask her to send out a replacement as soon as possible. I'm sure she'll be able to find someone suitable.'

He seemed to be taking it for granted that she would just meekly fall in with his plans for her rapid departure. Furious at the way she was being manipulated, she was about to launch into a heated argument when a shaft of common sense abruptly broke through all the hot anger. Slumping back in the chair, she briefly closed her eyes. What was the point in fighting tooth and nail to stay here? What would she gain in the end except a lot of extra pain? Okay, so it was going to be desperately painful to pack her bags and walk away from Kyle Allander, but it wasn't going to be any easier in a few weeks' time, when the book was finally finished. Better to go now, she reasoned with sudden weariness, not drag out the torment until it reached the point where it could easily break her in two.

Her shoulders drooped.

'All right,' she conceded defeatedly at last. 'Make whatever arrangements you like.'

'You won't regret this,' Sir Charles assured her. 'I'll make sure Miss Haversham knows that you didn't leave because we were displeased with your work. And, of course, I'll provide some financial compensation to make up for any inconvenience——'

'I don't want your money!' she threw at him furiously, her eyes suddenly sparking with pure contempt.

His face lost some of its florid colour. 'No, of course not,' he said hastily. 'Most tactless of me to offer.' He paused, went on more quietly, 'Lydia's all I have—her mother died years ago, and I've no other children. Yes, I spoil her, but it's only because I love her so much. Surely you can understand that? I'll do everything I can to give her what she wants. And right now, what she wants is Kyle Allander. I don't know how he feels about her, if the attraction's mutual or not, but I'll do whatever's necessary to give their relationship every possible chance to develop. If that means getting rid of every other attractive female for miles around, then I'll do just that if I possibly can. Kyle and Lydia must be allowed to spend these few days together without any distractions of any kind. I'm afraid you're just far too pretty, Miss Shepherd. I really can't allow you to stay here.'

Oddly, Carrie felt a strange pang of pity for this misguided man. 'You're making a mistake,' she told him, almost gently. 'You really aren't doing Lydia any favours by trying to make everything easy for her.'

Sir Charles shrugged helplessly. 'It's my way of showing my love for her,' he answered. 'Maybe one day, when you've got children of your own, you'll be able to understand.' He glanced at his watch. 'I must go. Thank you for being so co-operative, Miss Shepherd.'

After he'd left, Carrie stared at the typewriter, a heavy depression settling over her. One thing she was certain of. If she *did* ever have any children, she'd never, ever behave like Sir Charles, trying to fight all their battles for them. How awful it would be to have them turn out like Lydia Kingwood, a spoilt brat who rushed to Daddy every time she saw something she wanted, demanding that he get it for her, no matter what it cost in money or other people's feelings.

By the time she stumbled into bed that night, she felt totally drained. Almost instantly she dropped into a deep sleep, only finally waking up because someone was persistently shaking her.

'Carrie, are you awake?' asked Kyle's voice.

Kyle? No, it couldn't be. Yet those dark tones were quite unmistakable.

She blinked a couple of times.

'What are you doing here?' she mumbled rather incoherently. 'It's the middle of the night.'

'It's early morning,' he corrected her. 'And if you want to come with me, you'd better be ready in ten minutes.'

She rubbed her eyes, not quite sure she wasn't dreaming all of this.

'Come with you where?' she questioned sleepily.

'You'll find out later,' he answered evasively. Then he added a little roughly, 'It's—well, I hope it's something that'll help to make up for the rather lousy time you've had since you arrived here.'

Fully awake now, she stared up at him, but he was already moving away.

'Ten minutes,' he reminded her, then he quickly left the room.

Wondering what on earth was going on, she scrambled out of bed, hurried along to the bathroom for a quick wash, then struggled into some clean clothes. As she dragged a comb through her tousled hair, she peered at her reflection in the mirror and grimaced.

'No prizes for glamour,' she decided ruefully, and dabbed on a smattering of blusher, a thin coating of mascara, to try and improve matters. Then she trotted off to find Kyle, still wondering where they could possibly be going.

To her surprise, she found Sir Charles pacing up

and down the breakfast room, looking distinctly
unhappy.

'I don't really approve of this,' he grunted as she
came in.

Not having the slightest idea what he was
talking about, she didn't answer him. Instead, she
poured herself some coffee, and was about to grab
a slice of toast when Kyle strode in.

'No time for breakfast,' he instructed. 'We'll eat
later. We've got to leave now or we'll be late.'

'Late?' she echoed as he bustled both her and Sir
Charles out of the room. 'Late for what?'

'You're coming on this trip instead of Lydia,'
Sir Charles told her, disappointment—and disapproval—very evident in his voice. 'Kyle's idea,
not mine.'

'But *where* are we going?' she persisted in
exasperation.

'I think he wants it to be a surprise.'

'The surprise is that I'm somehow managing to
keep my temper,' she muttered under her breath.
'And why isn't Lydia coming?'

Kyle overheard that last question. 'The silly girl
lay out in the sun for too long,' he replied coolly.
'She's got heatstroke.'

'Shouldn't someone stay here and look after
her?' ventured Carrie, silently praying that no one
would nominate her for the job.

'Fergus will take care of her,' Kyle answered, to
her relief. 'She's not too bad, just a thumping
headache and very burnt skin. She'll be fine in a
day or two.'

At least that explained Sir Charles' gloomy
face, Carrie thought with an irrepressible surge of
pure glee. Lydia could hardly practice her vamp-
like charms on Kyle while glowing with painful
sunburn.

When they reached the Land Rover, Sir Charles rather pointedly got into the front with Kyle, leaving her to clamber into the back. She didn't mind. She could sit and study the back of Kyle's head; fix in her mind the exact way that silky black hair curled into the strong column of his neck; memorise the set of his shoulders, the supple movement of muscles as he expertly steered the Land Rover across the plains, obviously knowing exactly where he was going even though she was hopelessly lost as soon as the lodge disappeared from sight in the early morning gloom.

After they'd been travelling for a while, the sun came up with its usual swiftness. Carrie peered inquisitively ahead, her sharp eyes spotting a hint of movement on the far horizon. The Land Rover trundled steadily on and she finally made out a large truck, a Jeep, the figures of several men, and something square attached to a great sprawl of crumpled cloth or paper.

'Well?' prompted Kyle as they drew even nearer. 'Have you figured it out yet?'

Carrie stared in astonishment.

'It's a balloon,' she said at last. 'You're going up in a balloon.'

'*We're* going up in a balloon,' he corrected her gently.

Her stomach turned over.

'Are we?' she gulped.

'Sir Charles arranged this trip for himself and Lydia. There seemed no point in cancelling it just because Lydia was stupid enough to get heatstroke, so I persuaded Sir Charles to let you come along instead.'

And remembering her conversation with Sir Charles yesterday, Carrie could guess just how hard *that* must have been. Yet she also knew—to

her cost—how downright impossible it was to
deflect Kyle from a certain course of action once
he'd set his mind on it.

'But what's a balloon doing out here, in the
middle of nowhere?' she asked, puzzled.

'We're in one of the main tourist areas now,'
explained Kyle. 'Safari tours are becoming more
and more popular, and this is one more way to
view the animals, an alternative to bumping
around in a Land Rover or trekking around on
foot with one of the local guides.'

They were starting to inflate the balloon now
and Carrie jumped out of the Land Rover and
went over to watch, fascinated as a fierce tongue
of flame roared out of the burner, sending hot
air shooting into the huge envelope of thin
nylon. There was one white face among the
crowd of cheerful black ones, a tall, red-haired
man who was supervising the entire operation,
yelling orders in a mixture of languages but
obviously somehow succeeding in making himself
understood.

'Hallo, Kyle!' he shouted above the tumult of
the giant burner blasting the hot air into the
balloon. 'You've just timed it right, the weather's
perfect at the moment.'

'That's why we had to come so early,' Kyle
explained to Carrie, making her jump slightly as
he appeared at her side, tall and imposing even
among this crowd of strong-muscled, vigorous
men. 'Later on, when the sun's at full strength, the
hot air starts to rise and you get strong thermals,
which makes ballooning impossible. This early in
the morning there aren't any thermals and very
little wind, so conditions are ideal. By the way,' he
went on, gesturing at the red-haired man, 'that's
Dave Stanton. Like all balloonists, he's a little

mad, but there's no one else I'd trust to take me up in one of these fickle bubbles of air.'

'Are you calling my balloon names?' roared Dave, striding over and thumping Kyle on the back in greeting.

'Just explaining to Carrie why I had to drag her out of bed at the crack of dawn,' answered Kyle with a grin.

'How do we actually get up in the air?' asked Carrie with more than a touch of apprehension.

'That's easy,' Dave replied promptly. 'All those men hanging on to the basket just let go and whoosh, up we go.'

Carrie was beginning to wish she'd stayed in bed. 'And what happens once we're actually up there?'

'We go wherever the wind takes us,' Kyle told her. 'There's no steering, no brakes, we'll just drift along until it's time to come down again.'

She nibbled her lip nervously. 'I think that coming down worries me more than going up,' she admitted frankly.

'Nothing to worry about,' Dave reassured her. 'See that truck?' She glanced over at the ramshackle vehicle he was pointing to, then nodded. 'Well, Sirili, he's my head man, that tall one over there, he's going to follow us in that truck with the rest of the crew. When we come down, they'll all be waiting for us and we'll have a champagne breakfast. It'll be perfectly safe, I promise, I've been up hundreds of times and never had an accident. Well, only one or two,' he amended thoughtfully, 'there was that time when——'

'Enough!' interrupted Kyle, raising one black eyebrow warningly. 'You can tell us all the gory details *after* we're safely back on the ground again.'

'Okay,' grinned Dave. 'Excuse me, just got to see to the last few details.'

As he hurried back to his beloved balloon, Kyle absently ran his fingers through his shaggy hair. The early morning light was much brighter now, shining full on to those dominant features, and Carrie's brows drew together in a slightly alarmed frown as she noticed for the first time that his face was tinted with an unnatural pallor.

'Do you feel all right?' she asked a little anxiously.

'I'm fine,' he answered with a touch of brusqueness. 'Just a headache, that's all.' He paused, then added perceptively, 'Are you nervous about going up?'

'A little,' she admitted, feeling that tiny lurch in her stomach again as she stared, awestruck, at the nearly fully inflated balloon, towering high above them now, its nylon canopy glowing brightly in the sunlight.

'There's no danger,' he assured her. 'We used Dave's balloon several times when we were filming, for aerial shots, and he really does know what he's doing. You know that I wouldn't let you go anywhere near it if I thought there were any risk involved.'

His unexpected concern for her safety brought a funny tight feeling to her throat. She couldn't answer him, could only turn away and stare hard at the balloon with eyes that were suddenly blurred and prickly.

I shouldn't have come, she thought a little wildly. It was stupid, *stupid*. In a couple of days my replacement will be here and I'll be going back to England. If I'd an ounce of sense I'd have stayed well out of Kyle's way for the rest of my stay here.

Only this had all happened so quickly, she'd been dragged out of bed and brought here before she'd even had time to think what she was doing. Now they were going floating off in this balloon together and her head was shrieking that it was definitely *not* a good idea, but her heart wanted to go, wanted it so much, these few precious hours together, something to remember during all the lonely, lonely days that lay ahead.

'Hey, we're almost ready,' shouted Dave. 'Hop in quick, she's difficult to hold down once she's fully inflated.'

He was standing in the wicker basket, expertly using the burner to blast more hot air into the balloon so that the basket was now straining to leave the ground, only held down by the half-a-dozen men who were hanging on to its sides.

With some help from Kyle, Carrie scrambled over the side, blinking apprehensively as she felt the basket shift under her feet. Kyle lithely jumped in beside her, then glanced around.

'Where's Sir Charles?' he queried.

'Changed his mind about coming,' grinned Dave. 'He took one look at the balloon when it was inflated and got a bad attack of cold feet. One of my men is going to take him back to the lodge in the Jeep.' He gave another brief, noisy blast on the burner and Carrie's heart nearly stopped as she saw the fierce flames shooting up into the canopy.

'Are you sure it won't catch fire?' she muttered to Kyle, clutching fearfully at his arm.

'The bottom of the canopy has a skirt of fire-proof material,' he told her with a reassuring smile. 'There's absolutely no chance of it going up in flames.'

Feeling rather foolish, she hurriedly let go of his arm, quickly reminded herself that she shouldn't—

mustn't—touch him. Yet it was difficult to move around in the tiny basket without bumping into someone, and it always seemed to be Kyle with whom she was constantly coming into contact.

Another quick blast on the burner, then she could feel the balloon straining to go, almost as if it were alive, longing to soar up into the blue, blue sky, its natural element.

'Hands off!' shouted Dave, and the men who'd been holding on to the basket let go and suddenly they were rising, at first slowly, majestically, then the ground began to drop away at a faster speed, and for a few moments her stomach felt as if it were dropping with it. Then there was nothing but silence and the light brush of cool air against her face, and it was totally, absolutely marvellous.

Turning to Kyle, her exhilaration abruptly drained away as she saw that he looked even paler than when he'd been on the ground. There was nothing dull or colourless about his silver-grey eyes, though, quite the contrary, they positively glittered with almost feverish brilliance. Deep unease filled her as she looked at him and she was about to say something when Dave touched her arm.

'Down there,' he pointed, directing her attention to a small lake to their left.

Nearly half of it seemed to be carpeted in a pattern of pink and crimson, as if it were covered with hundreds, thousands of exotic tropical flowers. Then a pair of hyenas approached the lake, and the coloured carpet swirled up into the air, circling round the lake a couple of times before finally alighting again on the far side, a safe distance away from the hyenas.

'Flamingoes,' said Kyle, as fascinated as she was by the incredible sight. 'No matter how often you see them, you never quite get over how beautiful they are.'

His voice sounded quite steady and normal, so she decided not to comment on his worrying pallor. She guessed he was a man who wouldn't want a lot of fuss made if he were feeling a bit off-colour. Anyway, it was probably just that headache he'd mentioned earlier.

Her attention was soon seized by other things, and she eagerly drank in all the fascinating sights as they drifted silently along; three lionesses basking in the early morning sun, their cubs playing beside them; the ungainly yet oddly appealing wildebeestes with their long, mournful faces; hyenas and jackals scavenging around in the wake of the hunters of the night; even a glimpse of a cheetah prowling through the long grass, every detail of its beautifully marked coat clearly visible to the enthralled watchers floating overhead.

Carrie was so captivated that she hung rather precariously over the side of the basket, anxious not to miss one single thing. She was hardly aware of Kyle's restraining hand on her shoulder, at least not until another noisy blast from the burner broke through her concentration, abruptly snapping her back to reality. The balloon quickly gained more height, but for Carrie the spell was broken, the fascination of what was happening far below them shrivelling into insignificance against the sensation of those long, strong fingers lightly gripping her shoulder.

After that, nothing seemed of any importance except his nerve-shattering closeness. Useless to tell herself that there was no choice, that they were so cramped inside that small basket that they couldn't have avoided touching each other even if they'd wanted to. Every tiny movement of the basket seemed to bring some point of their bodies into contact, it was like a subtle form of torture that went on and on, thighs, knees, arms, shoulders, brief flash-points of pure sensation that tormented her nearly beyond bearing.

She actually gasped with relief when Dave called out that they'd be coming down soon. Nerve-ends so raw that she felt as if she'd been stripped of several layers of protective skin, she jumped visibly as Kyle took her hand to guide it to a small handle on the inside of the basket.

'Hold on to this as we land,' he instructed.

They were only a few yards off the ground by this time. Dave had picked out a flat, treeless area for their landing site, and had already thrown out the trail-rope, which dragged along the ground behind them and slowed the balloon still further. Then there were several teeth-rattling bumps and Kyle's arm locked tight around her waist, holding her steady until the basket was quite still. Dave had already pulled on the red line which opened a large section at the top of the canopy, releasing the hot air. As the huge canopy gracefully began to deflate and collapse, they climbed out of the basket, Kyle drawing Carrie to one side as Dave attended to his beloved balloon.

'Well, was it worth getting up a little early for?' he asked softly.

'Oh yes,' she breathed. 'It was fantastic.'

'And you weren't scared?'

'Certainly not! Well, perhaps a little, at the very beginning,' she admitted with a grin.

Dave glanced over his shoulder.

'I meant to tell you, Kyle, I spotted a new pack of wild dogs just to the north of here the other day. Only a small pack, four or five adults and a couple of half-grown pups, but I thought you'd like to know.'

'How far north?' asked Kyle, instantly interested.

'A few miles, but they were on the move. It looked as if they were heading towards those hills in the distance.' Dave turned his head, squinted in the other direction, where a cloud of dust was clearly visible. 'Here come the trucks,' he added with some satisfaction. 'They'll be here in a few minutes, then we can start on the champagne breakfast.'

'I'm not hungry,' Kyle answered. 'As soon as the Land Rover arrives I think I'll head north, see if I can find any trace of that pack you mentioned. Carrie, Dave will take care of you, take you back to the lodge after you've had breakfast.'

'Oh, I'm not hungry either,' she told him quickly, ignoring the rebellious grumbles of her stomach. 'Can't I come with you? After all, you might want to dictate some notes if you eventually catch up with those wild dogs.'

Even to her own ears it sounded a feeble excuse for going with him, and from the expression on his dark features it was clear he was going to turn her down flat. Just then, though, Dave intervened.

'I've really not got time to take Carrie back to the lodge,' he said rather apologetically. 'I've quite a lot of work to do on the balloon once we get back to base, and I've got to get it finished today. I've a group of tourists booked for an early morning flight tomorrow.'

At first, Kyle looked a little annoyed; then he rubbed his fingers fretfully over his forehead, as if his headache had just returned in full force. Finally, and with obvious reluctance, he nodded. 'All right, Dave, I know you have to run to a pretty tight schedule. Carrie can come with me.'

Carrie felt a great rush of relief, then hard on its

heels came a strange surge of defiance. Today was hers! It had just been given to her against all the odds, like an unexpected gift from the gods. There was no Lydia, no Sir Charles around to ruin it, she'd have Kyle all to herself for these last few precious hours. Okay, so going with him wasn't the most sensible thing she'd ever done, but just for once she was going to chuck common sense right out of the window. She intended to grab today and treasure it, lock every second of it away into her memory, a small insurance against all the empty tomorrows that loomed ahead of her.

The truck, which had been following the balloon at a distance, finally rumbled up to them, closely followed by Kyle's Land Rover, driven by one of Dave's men. Kyle walked over and took over the driving seat, as if impatient to be off, while Carrie hurriedly thanked Dave for the marvellous flight before scurrying after him.

Dave rummaged around in the back of his truck, then ran over to the Land Rover, shoved something on to the back seat.

'In case you get hungry later,' he grinned. 'Happy hunting.'

They drove in silence for quite a while, bumping their way over the plains towards the distant hills.

'Is it really so very important to find one small pack of wild dogs?' ventured Carrie finally.

'The problem is, they're in danger of disappearing completely,' Kyle explained. 'For years they were regarded as pests and shot indiscriminately. Now it's disease that seems to be the main problem, mainly distemper, the same disease that hits domestic dogs. If there is a new pack in the area then the first thing is to check if it's healthy.'

The Land Rover jolted violently as it hit a pothole and Carrie's next question flew completely out of her head. Instead, she clung grimly to her seat as Kyle drove on at his usual fast speed and yet without the skilful competence to which she'd become accustomed. A little belatedly, she realised that he didn't seem to be paying much attention to his driving. A couple of times she even caught his eyes drooping shut for a few seconds, as if they were just too heavy for him to keep open any longer. Then they would abruptly jerk open again, revealing a gaze that was becoming frighteningly over-bright and yet somehow glazed, not really focusing on anything, and certainly not on the uneven ground which they were now travelling over at a recklessly breakneck speed.

Something else she noticed. It was certainly getting warmer inside the Land Rover as the sun climbed higher into the sky, yet it wasn't unpleasantly hot so far, so why was Kyle's skin glistening with perspiration?

Her unease grew and deepened as they travelled on. Once, he actually seemed to fall asleep at the wheel, his eyes closing and not opening again until she anxiously shook his arm. And as she touched him, her eyes flew open very wide. His skin was burning hot, as if he were on fire inside. It was pretty clear he was starting to run a high fever.

Carrie gazed out of the window slightly frantically. It was so *empty* everywhere, not another human being in sight even though she could see for miles in all directions, no one who would come rushing to help them if anything happened.

Nothing's going to happen, she told herself firmly, trying to stop the panic from welling up and taking over completely. He's got a slight temperature, that's all. Probably some local fever he's picked up. Yet were such fevers dangerous? How did you treat them, how long did they last?

As her mind raced over all the unanswerable questions, she chewed her bottom lip worriedly, tried desperately to work out what she should do.

Another bone-jarring jolt resolved the problem. The first thing was to get him to stop this Land Rover before he killed both of them.

'I'm very hungry,' she said, fighting hard to keep her voice calm. 'Can't we stop for a while, have something to eat?'

Knowing how stubborn he could be, how determined he was to locate this new pack of wild dogs, she'd expected him to simply refuse her request outright. At first, though, he didn't even seem to hear it. And when she repeated it a second time, in a voice that had begun to quaver alarmingly, he just stared ahead for a few seconds, then gave a small shrug.

'If you like. I'm tired, I could do with a short rest.'

His own voice sounded strange, rather hoarse and slightly slurred. He steered the Land Rover towards a clump of trees, drove it into the patch of shade under their spreading branches, then cut the engine.

Carrie released a soft sigh of relief. Goal number one accomplished. Now goal number two had to be tackled. Yet how on earth was she going to persuade this maddeningly strong-willed man that he was in no fit state to drive any further? It certainly wasn't going to be easy!

First things first, she really was hungry now. Reaching over to the back seat, she found the small wicker hamper Dave had left there. Opening the lid, she blinked at the cold meat, fresh fruit— and the two bottles of champagne.

'I'm so thirsty!' muttered Kyle.

He grabbed one of the bottles of champagne, wrestled with the top, finally popped the cork, then drank in great, long gulps.

It seemed to revive him slightly. After he'd drained half the bottle, he glanced at her, raised one eyebrow in a rueful gesture.

'Sorry, I forgot my manners,' he apologised. He wiped the top of the bottle and handed it to her.

She swallowed a few mouthfuls, coughed a little as the bubbles danced their way down her throat, then handed it back to him. As she hungrily attacked the food, he drained the rest of the bottle, but didn't seem to want anything to eat.

Munching her way through the cold meat, Carrie pondered heavily over her main problem. How to persuade him that they had to turn round and head back to the lodge before his fever got worse?

Deciding that she might as well be blunt, tell him straight out that he just wasn't fit to drive any further, she took a deep breath and turned to him.

He'd fallen asleep. Sprawled out in the seat, his head was propped against one hand like a young child's.

'Not surprising, considering you drank a whole bottle of champagne,' murmured Carrie reprovingly. Yet a tiny smile touched the corners of her mouth as she studied him at his most vulnerable, letting her gaze slide slowly over the features that she already knew so well. The thick, black hair, the dark brows and long lashes, the fine mouth and the long, tanned line of his throat.

A small frown furrowed her forehead as, perturbed, she noticed other things. His too-fast breathing, the powerful chest rising and falling with disturbing speed, the dull flush of colour underlining the striking cheekbones, the damp patches of sweat on his shirt.

Perhaps it's nothing serious and he'll sleep it off, she told herself hopefully. A little voice inside her head told her she was only fooling herself, yet she stubbornly ignored it, and clung grimly to the hope that Kyle would be fine when he eventually woke up again.

Minutes crawled by, slowly stretching into hours. She ate some of the fruit, more to help pass the time than because she wanted it, then glanced at her watch for the hundredth time. Over three hours since he'd fallen asleep. The sun was high overhead now, it was stiflingly hot inside the Land Rover, even though they were shielded from the full force of the sun's rays by the shade of the branches overhead.

Reluctantly, Carrie reached a decision. They couldn't stay here any longer. She'd have to wake him, then somehow force him to see sense. They *had* to turn back. The wild dogs would just have to wait, he could go looking for them some other day.

She gripped his arm, then gave a tiny gasp. His skin was so hot, so dry, heat seemed to be pouring out of it in wave after wave. Fear surging up inside her, she shook him, called his name, softly at first, then with a more desperate urgency.

He didn't stir. The silver-grey eyes remained shut, no matter how hard she shook him. Then she started to tremble uncontrollably as the truth hit her with sickening force.

He wasn't asleep. He was unconscious!

CHAPTER EIGHT

How could a day that had started out so well have turned into such a nightmare? She slumped back into her seat, the fear gnawing at her insides now, seeming to be eating her up. They were such a long way from civilisation, she'd never felt so utterly isolated in her entire life, so totally helpless.

All she wanted to do was sit and howl her eyes out, weakly give in to the hysteria boiling up and up inside her. Instead, though, she somehow got a grip on herself, sat up, and roughly scrubbed the dampness from her eyes with the sleeve of her shirt.

'What the hell good is it going to do if you go to pieces?' she lectured herself angrily. 'You're the only chance Kyle's got of getting out of this mess. Use your brains, Carrie, don't sit here bawling like a stupid kid.'

It was fairly obvious that they couldn't stay here. No one would come looking for them for hours and hours. Dave would already have sent a message to the lodge saying that they'd set off on the trail of the wild dogs. No one would realise anything was wrong until late this evening, when they didn't return. Even then, it might be ages before anyone found them, and Kyle needed help *now*.

Forcing her confused, scared brain to work, she shakily made her first decision. She had to get Kyle into the passenger seat so that she could drive the Land Rover. The trouble was, she had no idea in which direction she should head, she'd become totally disorientated during that long, bumpy ride. Surely if she just kept on driving, though, she'd eventually find someone who would help them?

Grimly ignoring the fact that it was possible to drive for hours in this wild and desolate land without meeting anyone at all, she concentrated on trying to shift Kyle's limp body out of the driving seat.

'Oh, won't you wake up for just a couple of minutes?' she muttered despairingly, hauling futilely at one heavy arm, spurred on to fresh efforts by that alarming fire burning just underneath his skin, the frightening hoarseness of his breathing.

As if in answer to her muttered entreaty, he stirred slightly, although his eyes remained tightly shut.

'Carrie,' he murmured thickly. 'My lovely, lovely Carrie——'

Her heart seemed to stop beating for several seconds and a sudden heat ignited deep inside her, a fever fierce enough to match his own.

Stop it! she ordered herself sharply. Concentrate on practical problems. This is no time for silly fantasies.

'Kyle!' she said with new urgency, leaning over him. 'Can you hear me? You've got to move. Listen to me, you *must move*.'

He lifted his head slightly, although his eyes remained shut.

'So hot,' he muttered.

She knew that, could feel those terrifying waves of heat rolling off him.

'Come on,' she coaxed, tugging at him vigorously, 'you've got to help me get you into the other seat. I can't move you on my own, you're too heavy. Just try and make an effort, please, Kyle, *try*!'

He seemed to respond more to the sound of her voice than her physical efforts to move him. Encouraged by that, she kept on talking, babbling away, not even knowing what she was saying, just praying that he'd hang on to consciousness long enough to do what she wanted.

It seemed to take forever, but at last he was in the passenger seat, leaving her free to wriggle behind the wheel. Gasping with strain, sweat dripping freely off her now after the sheer physical work involved in helping to move that powerful body, she brushed the damp hair out of her eyes, then reached for the ignition with trembling fingers.

She'd never driven a Land Rover before. The gears grated horribly as she tried to sort them out. Finally, though, the Land Rover was moving slowly across the grassy plains. After a moment's thought, she decided to head towards the hills that shadowed the horizon. They were the only positive landmarks in the sea of grass, stunted trees and rocky outcrops, and surely she'd find some signs of life once she got there? Good heavens, this was a fast-developing tourist area, safari holidays were becoming more and more popular, lodges and safari camps were springing up all over the place. All she had to do was to find one, then everything would be all right.

Her gaze slewed round anxiously as she drove along, searching for any sign of human life. Nothing! And the afternoon heat kept growing fiercer and fiercer, her own clothes were sticking damply to her body so she could hardly bear to think what Kyle must be going through as his temperature roared even higher. There wasn't anything she could do about it, though, except try and get him to a place where medical help would be available.

The hills seemed rather nearer now, their hazy blue outline patterning the skyline. She was getting tired, very tired, but she ignored her fatigue, didn't think of stopping until her gaze flickered over the fuel gauge.

It was hovering on the empty mark. The discovery sent an unpleasant jolt of shock through her, galvanising her into a few minutes of furious thinking. Should she keep going until she ran right out of petrol, gambling wildly on finding help at the very last moment? Or would it be better to stop now, where she could at least choose a suitable spot?

A quick glance at Kyle's flushed skin convinced her that it would be downright dangerous to get stranded out here in the open. He was already burning up. He needed to be kept as cool as possible, not explosed to the full heat of the sun.

Ahead of her was a fairly high, sprawling outcrop of rock, one side already in shadow as the sun began to sink slightly in the sky. Aiming the Land Rover in that direction, she gave a small sigh of relief as she finally drove into its shadow, away from those killing rays of the sun. She cut the engine, then turned anxiously to Kyle.

To her surprise, his eyes were open, although they didn't seem to be focusing on anything. It was strange—and terrifying—to see that shrewdly intelligent gaze so blank, so unseeing.

'Thirsty,' he mumbled.

She hastily reached for the second bottle of champagne, struggled for a couple of minutes with the cork and finally managed to remove it.

'Is champagne good for someone with a fever?'

she worried out loud to herself as she helped him
to swallow a few mouthfuls. 'There's nothing else,
though.'

After he'd finished drinking, she sipped a couple
of mouthfuls herself, just enough to wet her dry
mouth and throat. Although ragingly thirsty, she
didn't dare drink more. Her knowledge of fevers
was sketchy, to say the least, but she was sure it
was important to maintain a steady intake of
liquid. He was sweating so much that he'd soon
become dehydrated if he didn't drink fairly
steadily. And all she had was the champagne, so
she had to save it for him, somehow try not to
think about her own craving for a long drink.

The afternoon crawled by, the shadows began to
lengthen. Although it was a relief that the
blistering heat was fading, Carrie viewed the night
ahead with equal trepidation. Once the sun went
down, the heat of the day would give way to a
bone-chilling cold, and it didn't need much
medical knowledge to know what harm that would
do to someone in Kyle's condition.

She briefly closed her eyes, feeling the old
despair fighting its way up again, making her dry
throat ache with tension. If only there was
something she could *do*, she felt so damned
helpless just sitting here like this.

With a shaky sigh, she dragged her heavy eyes
open again, knowing it was time to try and
persuade Kyle to take another drink. Then her
breath caught in her throat, a tiny squeak of alarm
escaped her.

They were no longer alone. Standing just in
front of the Land Rover was a tall, imposing
figure, absolutely still as a statue. Thin, handsome, his hair braided and coloured with red
ochre, wearing a toga-like garment which fastened

over one shoulder and left the other one bare, he gazed directly at Carrie's terrified face with a dark, unblinking stare.

Her own gaze shifted slightly, fixing on the spear which he held in his hand. All sorts of wild fears leapt through her confused mind and her teeth started to chatter noisily.

The figure moved, took a couple of strides forward, causing Carrie to huddle tremulously in her seat. Her vivid imagination ran riot as her eyes fixed on that long, lethal spear which he gripped so expertly in his strong, black fingers.

'W-What do you want?' she stammered in a quavering voice.

He put his head slightly on one side, studied her with all the fascination of a child discovering a new toy. Then he said something in a language which was totally incomprehensible to her, and she shook her head despairingly.

'I don't understand,' she moaned.

Fear was retreating a little now, though, and in its place was stirring a dim flicker of memory. She stared at him again, saw his proud bearing, his distinctive aquiline face, and was suddenly sure she knew who he was. One of the Maasai, a semi-nomadic tribe who lived in this part of the world, moving around from area to area as they grazed their herds of cattle, their most prized possession.

New hope surged inside her.

'My friend—he's sick,' she said urgently. 'Can you help him?'

She leant to one side so that he could see Kyle. Although the Maasai obviously hadn't understood a word she had said, he leant forward and peered at Kyle for some time, intently studying him and at the same time muttering to himself softly.

At last he seemed to reach some kind of a

decision. Straightening up again, he turned his
back on her, began to walk away from the Land
Rover. Terrified that he was just going to leave her
there, Carrie was about to call after him when he
half-turned, made an imperious gesture with his
head.

The message was clear. He wanted her to follow
him.

Shaking with relief, she switched on the engine,
prayed that there'd be enough petrol to take them
wherever he was leading them. It was like a
dream, she mused dazedly as the Land Rover
bumped along slowly in first gear. That tall, dark,
arrogant figure with the spear, the golden rays of
the dying sun, the sick man sprawled beside her—
none of it seemed quite real.

To her surprise, they didn't have far to go. The
Maasai led her round to the other side of the high
outcrop of rock and there, surrounded by an
encircling fence of thorn-bushes, were half-a-dozen
low huts.

The Maasai led her through a gap in the thorn-
fence, and immediately the Land Rover was
surrounded by an inquisitive crowd, many of them
women wearing wide, beautiful collars of brightly
coloured beads, with more beads in bands around
their foreheads. Explanations seemed to be made at
great speed, then the door of the Land Rover was
opened, Kyle was helped out and taken into a
small hut on the far side of the cleared space inside
the enclosure. Carrie guessed that the hut was
disused at the moment because it was in a fairly
poor state of repair, although some attempt at
patching it seemed to have been made fairly
recently.

Struggling to follow him, she was hampered by
the women, who seemed fascinated by her blonde

hair, touching it and grinning, all the while chattering away to her in their strange tongue. By the time she managed to reach the hut, she found someone had already fetched some animal skins for Kyle to lie on and one of the women was beginning to light a fire in the centre of the hut.

It was fairly dark inside and smelt—well, strange, Carrie conceded with a small wrinkling of her nose. But at least it would shelter them for the night and perhaps these people would know where to find a doctor—if she ever succeeded in making them understand what a doctor was. There was definitely going to be a communication problem.

She knelt beside Kyle, touched his forehead, and was filled with new apprehension as she felt its scorching heat. Then she gradually became aware that the chattering all around her had died down. Raising her head, she found that an older man had just entered the hut. His tightly curled hair was grey, his eyes strangely wise as he looked first at her, then at Kyle.

Then he bent over Kyle and seemed to be studying him with great intent. He prodded him a couple of times, made several brief, incomprehensible comments, and Carrie realised, a little deliriously, that Kyle was getting the Maasai equivalent of a full medical examination.

At last, the old man straightened up, said something at length to his respectful audience, who all nodded enthusiastically, apparently in complete agreement with his diagnosis.

Carrie was beginning to feel slightly hysterical. What next? Would he rattle some bones over Kyle, like an old-fashioned witch-doctor?

She soon found out. One of the women came in several minutes later with some dark liquid in a small bowl. Carrie stared at it suspiciously, then swivelled round to face the old man.

'What is it?' she demanded. 'What are you going to do with that?'

She soon found out. The old man took the bowl, held it to Kyle's dry lips, and had already persuaded him to drink a couple of mouthfuls before she came to her senses.

'No!' she yelled in sudden terror. 'You could be poisoning him!'

Frantically, she tried to knock the bowl out of the old man's hand, but a couple of the women caught hold of her thrashing arms, made soothing noises as she struggled to get free again.

'You don't understand,' she almost sobbed. 'He isn't used to your medicines, they could kill him!'

It was too late, the bowl was empty. The Maasai began to file out of the hut, apparently satisfied that they'd done all that was necessary, leaving Carrie to slump down defeatedly beside Kyle. Shakily, she stroked the damp strands of his hair, numbly wondering if she could bear to go on if he no longer existed in this world.

His fever raged all through the night and on through the next day. At regular intervals the Maasai women brought more small bowls of whatever the old man had given Kyle last night and Carrie didn't try to stop them any more. Whatever it was, it hadn't killed him, and who knew? It might even help. Certainly *she* couldn't do anything for him, except stay constantly at his side. Let them try to cure him with their herbs and whatever else they'd mixed into that dark potion. She was desperate enough now to try anything.

That second night in the Maasai encampment, they left her with a supply of wood to keep the small fire in the centre of the hut burning through

the night. There would have been a terrible smoky
fug in the hut if it hadn't been for those holes in
the roof, still waiting to be repaired. The smoke
drifted out through the holes, but unfortunately so
did much of the heat. Kyle had a couple of covers
to help keep him warm, but as the chill of the
night closed in around them, there was only one
way she could help protect him from the ravages
of the cold. As she'd done last night, she crept in
beside him, curling her body against his, sharing
her own warmth with him.

It was a queer, almost painful pleasure to lie
with him like this. She'd lain awake all through
last night, listening to his breathing, feeling the
quick thudding of his heart, and it had been
almost like sharing his most intimate secrets.
Tonight, though, she was tired, so very tired. She'd
been awake for over thirty-six hours, her eyes
simply wouldn't stay open even though she longed
to savour this illicit closeness, not lose one single
second of it.

She dozed for a while, finally waking up again
late into the night to find that the fire had burnt
very low. Carefully, she disentangled herself from
the sleeping man beside her, to put some more
sticks on the fire until the flames danced brightly
again and gentle warmth radiated towards them.
Then she slipped back into her nook at Kyle's side,
fitting herself into the curves of his body,
astonished all over again at how perfectly they
matched, as if specially designed to fit together like
this.

Kyle's voice murmured in her ear.

'Why are we sharing the same bed, Carrie?' And
while she was still recovering from the shock of
hearing him speak, he added blankly, 'And where
the hell are we?'

She propped herself up on one elbow to stare down at him anxiously. His face was clearly illuminated by the firelight; he looked tired and drained, but those startling silver-grey eyes were absolutely lucid for the first time since the fever had hit him. A glorious wave of relief nearly flattened her. The fever had broken. He wasn't going to die!

His gaze was still fixed on her, looking partly puzzled, partly—A slow wave of heat rolled over her as she realised what else she could see in his eyes.

Hurriedly, she began to explain what had happened, where they were, the garbled words pouring nervously out of her, but he seemed to be only half-listening. Hardly able to believe that the fever had really broken, that the crisis had passed, she pulled back the covers a few inches, ran her fingers lightly, shakily, over his skin.

It was cool to the touch, felt supple again instead of unnaturally dry.

He stared down at himself. 'Who undressed me?' he enquired with some interest.

Embarrassment instantly burned through her. 'I did,' she mumbled. 'I had to sponge you down several times when you were so hot. I left your underwear on, though,' she added hastily. 'You're perfectly decent.'

One black eyebrow lifted in a familiar, sardonic gesture and she wanted to weep with relief that he was his old mocking self again. Instead, she just blinked hard several times, and half-turned away from him.

His hand touched her arm.

'You haven't answered my original question,' he reminded her. 'Why are we sleeping in the same bed? Or what passes for a bed,' he added, looking

down with a touch of amusement at the animal
skins on which he was lying.

'To help keep you warm. I was so afraid you'd
develop pneumonia if you got cold.'

His eyes glittered as something stirred to life in
their depths.

'I'm not entirely recovered yet,' he reminded her
slightly huskily. 'Perhaps you'd better get right
back into bed with me. You don't want me to have
a relapse, do you?'

She hesitated momentarily, then realised he was
right. He was a very long way from being fully
recovered and the night *was* chilly. Taking a deep
breath, she slid back down beside him, to give a
small involuntary shudder as his arm came round
her.

'I feel strange,' he mused, 'almost as if I'm
dreaming. And I'm so damned weak. I've hardly
enough energy to move my little finger.' He
paused, to continue in a very different tone of
voice, 'Yet parts of me don't feel weak at all,
Carrie. How do you explain that?'

The breath sighed gently in her throat. 'You've
been very ill, you must still be feverish,' she
whispered, feeling strangely weak herself.

His fingers moved in a light caress, then rested
against her flat stomach.

'I've had a fever ever since I first set eyes on
you,' came his murmured confession. He found
her hand, pulled it towards him, imprisoned it
against the hot pulse of his body. 'Can't you feel
how I burn?' he muttered, in a suddenly
roughened voice.

Something jumped inside her, jumped again,
and she closed her eyes very tight, trying to push
all the crazy thoughts out of her spinning head.

'Kyle, this is insane. You're sick——'

'Then make me well,' he coaxed persuasively. 'You're the only one who can do it, Carrie. Only you'll have to help me, I haven't the strength to do it all on my own. Not this time——'

The fire crackled, sent a small flame leaping into the air. The brightness reflected in his eyes where another, very different fire burnt fiercely, unquenchably.

'Why don't you undress yourself, Carrie?' he challenged softly.

Oh God, this was mad! Yet that velvet voice was such a potent force, it overrode all her willpower, drained away the last dregs of her resistance. With fascinated horror, she found her hands were already stealing up to her shirt, sliding the buttons out of the button-holes.

'Slowly,' he instructed, his breath coming more and more unevenly now. 'There's no need to hurry. Not yet.'

Moving as if in a hypnotic trance, she obeyed him. As she slowly stripped, he drew back the covers, allowing her to see the gold lines of his body.

Carrie caught her breath. He was so beautiful! All supple lines, powerful curves, male potency. It made her want to cry with awe and delight.

'Just sit there for a moment,' he directed huskily as she reached her undies. 'Let me look at you.'

As she obeyed, the silver gaze flared restlessly, she saw the effort he had to make to control himself. The same firelight that gilded his body emblazoned her own, creating shadows in the hollows, touching the curves with subtle highlights. Her white bra and pants contrasted provocatively with the soft tones of her skin, and she saw a flush of colour creep along his high cheekbones, a flush that had nothing at all to do with his illness.

He reached up with one hand, and snapped open the tiny catch at the front of her bra. The cotton material fell away, the straps slithered down from her shoulders; then his fingers were brushing the full undersides of her breasts, gently, tantalisingly, as if he wanted to savour this moment, spin it out until neither of them could bear it an instant longer. Then his thumb slid up, touched the hard, throbbing peak, and both of them shuddered simultaneously.

'Come closer,' he ordered softly. Her entire body shaking from that one light, lethal touch, she slid down beside him, waiting breathlessly for his hand to continue its pattern of devastating caresses.

Instead, though, he stared at her, steadily held her gaze.

'Now I want you to take your pants off, Carrie,' came his quiet instruction. The silver gaze pierced right through her as he added provocatively, 'And mine.'

Confusion instantly rushed over her, threatening to swallow her up. Oh, damn her inexperience!

'I can't,' she stuttered a little frantically. 'I just can't. I n-never have——'

Her voice broke up completely, trailed away into fraught silence.

'I know you haven't,' he assured her soothingly. 'That's why I want you to do it now. I don't want you to be afraid of me, Carrie, I don't want my body to be a mystery to you. You're only nervous because you're entering an unknown land. Just take my hand and we'll explore it together. There's absolutely nothing to fear. All you have to do is trust me.'

Her bout of nerves rapidly died away; she *did* trust him. His gaze held on to hers, constantly

assuring her that she could come to no harm in his
arms, and with sudden boldness she slipped off her
panties, feeling a strange surge of confidence at her
own nakedness. Then, a little hesitantly, she laid
her hands on his body, felt his instant reaction to
her touch, a flare of response that danced through
his fever-weakened limbs, giving him new strength.

Exultancy shot through her, a burst of sheer
feminine vanity. This man wanted her, wanted *her*,
Carrie Shepherd! The knowledge caused something
to melt deep inside her, a small ball of fire blazed
gloriously into life, the flames ran along all her
nerve-ends until she burned from head to toe.

Could he see the flames? She was sure that he
could, not with his eyes but with that strange sense
of inner perception that marked him out from
other men, made him utterly unique.

With new found confidence, her fingers danced
over his shoulders, luxuriously buried themselves
in the light coating of hair on his chest, silently
admired the strong rib cage, the supple line of his
hips. Then they shamelessly brushed against the
waistband of his pants and an involuntary grunt
sounded deep in his throat.

His fingers shot up, began to caress the full
curve of her breast in a rhythmic movement that
left her gasping with delight. Then one hand slid
behind the nape of her neck, pulled her head down
to his so that his mouth could luxuriously explore
hers for a couple of long, delicious minutes. As if
belonging to someone else, her own hands crept
back to his waist again, drifted still lower ... she
heard the breath whistle jerkily out of his lungs,
felt him raise his hips so she could slide off the
constricting pair of pants. The thin material
slipped easily over the curved swell of his buttocks,
then down the long line of his legs, her inner wrists

brushing against the strong muscles of his thighs, the sleekness of his calves. The breath panted softly in her throat, she was flying straight into a new world, a magic world, dizzy with the sensation of warm skin meeting warm skin, rubbing together in mutual arousal, touching in soft, nerve-stripping gestures of love and need.

All fear, all awkwardness had dropped away, her body silently sang its longing to know everything about him, to revel in his total maleness. She explored with new boldness, unravelling the mysteries of his body, marvelling at his shuddering responsiveness to her questing fingers. Then an ache began to build inside her, nurtured by the lethal skill of his oh-so-experienced hands until she shivered under its force. Almost groaning in protest at the pleasure he was forcing on her, she then gasped in disbelieving ecstasy as his tongue flickered against her softness, sucking her down and down into a realm where pleasure reigned supreme and two souls could be welded into one by the incandescent heat of desire.

Blindly responding, she ran her hands over and over his hot, damp skin until he quivered with pent-up need. His fingers dug deeply, almost bruisingly into her delicate skin as he fought back the explosive force gathering inside him.

'Do you know how often I've wanted you to touch me like this?' he muttered thickly. 'How many nights I've lain awake aching for those pretty fingers against my flesh?'

'Tell me?' she breathed invitingly, loving the sound of his voice as it whispered in her ear.

'Every night since you arrived,' came his hoarse confession. 'God,' he added helplessly, 'I *must* be feverish or I wouldn't be telling you all these things.'

'I thought you didn't like blondes,' she

reminded him, innocently teasing him with her words and her fingers simultaneously until he groaned in protest.

'No more, Carrie, not unless you want to kill me with pleasure.' He paused, suddenly yawned. 'And as for not liking blondes,' he went on slightly sleepily, 'I like this particular blonde far too much. Far too much——'

He yawned again, almost convulsively, and his wandering hands became still, as if the effort of moving them was suddenly quite beyond him. Totally receptive to every response of his body, Carrie sensed the exhaustion that had welled up from nowhere and was now rolling over his fever-weakened body in huge waves, flattening his frail reserves of energy.

'Sorry,' came his apologetic and frustrated mutter as he buried his head against her shoulder. 'I still want you, but I don't think I can—I'm so tired, so very, very tired——'

With a new mature understanding, Carrie slid her arms around him, snuggling closer so that there was shared warmth, shared breathing, shared heartbeat.

'It doesn't matter,' she whispered comfortingly.

'Does matter,' he insisted in a voice now slurred with irresistible sleepiness. 'Does matter. But I can't——'

His voice trailed away as his eyes drooped shut, didn't open again. That unfamiliar, sensual ache still throbbed inside her, but she ignored it, it wasn't important. Seconds later, Kyle was deeply asleep, slipping back into unconsciousness as abruptly as he'd awakened out of it. Only this time it was a healthy, healing sleep, his body totally relaxed as it curled against hers, his breathing slow and even.

It was strange, but lying with him like this was somehow even more intimate than if they had actually made love. Naked and vulnerable, he slept in her arms as peacefully as a child, and she didn't move a muscle for fear of disturbing him. The last hours of the night drifted by, each one of them a small, personal treasure to prize, and it wasn't until the first light of dawn began to filter into the hut that she gave a tiny sigh and crept carefully out of his arms. Soon one of the Maasai women would be coming to check on the progress of their patient, and so she quickly dressed, her skin flushing with colour as she put on the clothes which she'd so wantonly taken off last night for Kyle's pleasure.

He slept on right through the morning, sprawled out on the makeshift bed, his dark tousled head resting against his arm. Carrie hovered anxiously around the entrance to the hut, feeling inexplicably nervous. What would happen when he finally woke up? Surely after last night everything *had* to be different, he *had* to have changed his mind about the way she fitted into his life? All the barriers between them had come tumbling down as he'd drawn her slowly but inexorably into that sensual whirlpool. Okay, so he'd left her whizzing dizzily round the edge, too weak from the fever to drag her right down to the exquisite depths, but that hadn't mattered, in a queer way it had made her feel even closer to him.

It was past midday when Kyle finally stirred. Stretching his long limbs so that the powerful muscles stood out in sharp relief, he grunted, opened his eyes. Then that silver gaze steadily darkened in growing puzzlement.

'Carrie?' he muttered, his black brows drawing

together broodingly. 'What the hell's happened? Where *are* we?'

What on earth was he talking about? Her heart began to thud so hard that she swayed a little, she was beginning to feel as if someone were squeezing her in a giant bear-hug. Her chest ached, the breath was wheezing in her constricted lungs and huge alarm bells were starting to clang frantically inside her head. He couldn't have forgotten last night, he *couldn't*. Yet she'd already told him where they were, how they'd got here, she'd explained everything when he'd first come out of that fever last night. Only now he couldn't remember any of it.

He was still staring at her in that rather confused, bewildered way and she wanted to scream at him to stop it, force him to remember. Instead, though, she somehow dragged her raw nerves under control, grimly fought to come to terms with the paralysing truth. The last couple of days must be a total blank in his memory! As far as he was concerned, last night had never happened.

Realising how alarming he must be finding it to have a gaping hole in his memory, she twisted her badly shaking fingers together, and somehow managed to speak.

'You—you've been very ill,' she choked in a low voice. 'A bad fever. You blacked out in the Land Rover after the balloon trip. Luckily, a Maasai found us, brought us here to his village. They've been treating you with some kind of herbal medicine——'

He ran his fingers through his tangled black hair.

'I've no idea what they gave me, but it seems to have cured me. Perhaps they ought to patent it, they'd probably make a fortune. How long have I been here? A few hours?'

She shook her head numbly.

'Since the day before yesterday,' she whispered.

That clearly shook him.

'The last thing I remember is sitting in the Land Rover and feeling so ill I wanted to die,' he recalled wryly. 'After that, nothing—except——' He frowned, seemed to be digging deep into his memory.

Hope briefly flared inside her.

'Except?' she prompted in a taut voice, all her nerves so highly strung that she thought they might fly apart at any moment.

'Oh, nothing,' he said casually. 'Just a lot of weird, jumbled dreams. I suppose I was delirious.'

For a moment, she nearly flung herself at him, shook him, screamed out the truth. Then her body slumped, the last dregs of hope quietly draining away. She was utterly empty inside now, as if her very soul had dissolved into the air and drifted away on the breeze.

Time to face the truth, she told herself dully. He didn't remember last night, chances were he was never going to remember it. And that meant nothing had changed between them. Those few hours in his arms had been an illusion, a bright, golden dream, but she should have known it was too beautiful to last. Now the dream was over, and she'd damned well better start picking up the pieces of her life or this was going to break her right in two.

'Yes,' she confirmed in a tight voice, 'you must have been delirious.' She shook her head, added in a low mutter, 'Perhaps we both were.'

He glanced up at her curiously. 'Have you been ill, too?'

'Nothing that I won't get over, in time.' She moved away, abruptly turned her back on him. If he saw her face, he'd want to know why her eyes were glistening so brightly.

Then, suddenly, she couldn't stand to be near him any longer. Something seemed to be tearing apart inside her and he was just lying there, letting it happen, and she hated him for it, *hated* him . . .

Spinning round, she dashed out of the hut, began running and running as if Kyle were the devil himself and were about to rise up from his sick bed to come pounding after her.

CHAPTER NINE

SHE didn't stop running until she cannoned into something warm and solid. Arms came out, wrapped themselves around her and held her tight.

'Carrie, what on earth's the matter?' demanded Simon's concerned voice.

Numbly she raised her head, the breath still wheezing in her lungs, her legs shaking with reaction.

'Simon?' she said dazedly. Then, seeing the man beside him, 'And Fergus?'

'In person,' agreed Fergus. 'And we're both pretty pleased to see you. Where's Kyle?'

She gestured towards the hut.

'He's—he's been ill, some kind of fever, but I think he's much better this morning.'

'We've been searching all over the place for you,' exclaimed Simon. 'Then a local pilot reported seeing a Land Rover in one of the Maasai camps in this area, so we headed straight over.'

Fergus was studying her pale, strained face with some concern. 'Why don't you go and sit in the Land Rover?' he suggested. 'We'll go and fetch Kyle, then we can drive back to the lodge.'

'It's run out of petrol,' she told them tiredly.

'That's all right,' Simon nodded, 'we've brought several spare cans with us in the Jeep. Leave it all to us, Carrie, we'll take care of everything now. You've obviously had a rough couple of days.'

Rough? she thought tiredly. That seemed something of an understatement. She didn't want to think about it any more, though. Trudging over

170

to the Land Rover, she opened the door, slumped into the front seat, closed her aching eyes.

Some time later, Simon climbed in beside her. 'I've refilled the tank. We can go now.'

'What about Kyle?' she forced herself to say.

'Still weak as a kitten, but fighting it all the way,' he answered cheerfully. 'He's travelling in the Jeep, with Fergus. Insisted on walking to the Jeep, even though his legs were wobbling like unset jellies. You know Kyle once he's made up his mind to do something, though.'

'Yes, I know Kyle,' she echoed painfully, and treacherous pictures danced through her whirling mind, vivid snatches of memory that brought with them a special ache that was fiercer than any physical injury.

'You don't look at all well, Carrie,' Simon remarked worriedly. 'I hope you're not going down with the same fever as Kyle.'

'I'm fine,' she muttered, 'just tired, that's all. Would you mind if we didn't talk? I've an awful headache.'

'Close your eyes and try to sleep,' he suggested sympathetically. 'We've a long drive ahead of us.'

Obediently, she closed her eyes, although she knew she wouldn't sleep. At least it meant she didn't have to make any effort to keep up a normal conversation, though. She liked Simon, she didn't want to hurt his feelings, but she just wasn't up to talking to anyone at the moment.

As the Land Rover bumped its way along, it took all her energy to fight off the idiotic impulse to rush straight to Kyle as soon as they reached the lodge, blurt out the truth, tell him everything—*everything*—that had happened in the Maasai village. Then she sighed softly. Don't be stupid, Carrie, she berated herself silently. What use would it be? And anyway, she reminded herself bitterly, exactly what would she tell him? That he'd wanted to make love to her? There was nothing new in that. He'd wanted her before. The only difference was, he'd always had the strength to draw back before, shying away from any serious involvement. Last night, with all his defences flattened because of the debilitating effects of the fever, he'd simply been too weak to fight his desire. That didn't mean he'd still want her today, she reminded herself dully. At least, not on a permanent basis. And the sooner she got that basic fact into her thick head, the sooner she'd start to get over this mad infatuation.

Only it wasn't infatuation, that was the trouble, she conceded with utter weariness as her thoughts chased themselves round and round in endless circles. In a way, she almost wished it were. A simple case of hero-worship would have been so much easier to have dealt with—and it wouldn't have hurt so damned much, as if someone had just ripped her guts out.

It was late evening before they reached the lodge. Kyle was hustled directly off to bed and Lydia instantly appointed herself as his personal nurse, declaring that no one else was to go anywhere near Kyle's room. She stared directly at Carrie as she made this announcement, but Carrie didn't even bother to argue. Let Lydia amuse herself by practising her wiles on Kyle. She'd get no further than any other female. Kyle was the original cat who walked by himself. He'd long ago mapped out the solitary pattern of his life and he was utterly determined to stick to it. Not even the sultry Lydia would be able to change his mind about that.

Exhausted beyond belief, yet knowing she

wouldn't be able to sleep, she pulled on a thick jumper, wandered restlessly out on to the dark verandah, suddenly craving solitude. When she heard footsteps behind her, for an instant her stomach jumped, her nerves stupidly tightened. Whirling round, she went dead inside again as she found herself facing Sir Charles.

'Ah, there you are, Miss Shepherd. I know you've had a very tiring day, but I wonder if I might have a brief word with you?'

His formal tone should have warned her, yet it didn't. She was incapable of thinking straight at that moment, she just wanted him to say whatever he had to say, then go away and leave her alone again.

'What do you want?' she asked, her voice quite expressionless.

'I've been in touch with the Haversham Agency,' he said, 'and as usual they've been very efficient. Your replacement arrives tomorrow morning. I thought I ought to let you know, as you'll no doubt want to return to London straight away.'

It was almost the final blow. She reeled briefly under it, then somehow collected herself together again.

'I didn't think—I wasn't expecting it to be so soon,' she stammered numbly.

'There was no reason for any delay, was there?' asked Sir Charles smoothly.

'No—no, I suppose not——'

All the same, she couldn't quite take it in.

'If you're packed and ready to leave in the morning, Simon can drive you to the airstrip and you can fly out on the same plane which is bringing in your replacement,' Sir Charles went on, in a tone which clearly told her that he expected her to fall in with these arrangements.

For a moment, quick anger swept through her. How dare he try and organise her life in this way! Then the anger swiftly died, and in its place came a queer apathy and the realisation that it would be far better like this, to go now, and quickly, before any more damage was done to her badly torn emotions.

Her head bowed in tired acquiescence.

'I'll be ready,' she told him in a flat tone.

'Splendid,' said Sir Charles with obvious relief. 'As a matter of fact, Fergus is taking Kyle to the local mission hospital in the morning, for a thorough check-up. By the time he gets back, you'll be gone and your replacement will be installed.'

'You've got it all worked out, haven't you?' she accused with a quick flash of resentment.

'I haven't tried to deceive you, Miss Shepherd,' Sir Charles answered steadily. 'I've already told you exactly why I'm doing this. I hope that, once you've left, Kyle will spend some time with my daughter, that perhaps he'll come to return her— well, her rather obvious affection for him.'

On the very point of losing her temper completely, Carrie suddenly shrugged defeatedly. What was the point? He was just a doting father indulging the whims of a hopelessly spoilt child. And whatever his motives for wanting to get rid of her, in the end they weren't really important. It would be better for everyone if she went straight back to England—including herself. And if she left in the morning, while Kyle was visiting the hospital, at least she wouldn't have to face the ordeal of saying goodbye to him.

'Don't worry, I'll catch that plane,' she confirmed in a low, bitter voice.

'I'm glad you're being sensible about this,' Sir

Charles said with some satisfaction. Then he went inside, leaving her alone on the unlit verandah.

She stared blindly out at the black shadows of the plains, remembering something that Kyle had said to her not so very long ago.

'The night is dark.'

And so it was. Tonight, and tomorrow night, and all the long, long nights as far ahead as she could see.

Miss Haversham couldn't quite hide her shock when she saw Carrie's face.

'Good heavens, have you been ill? That wretched climate, I suppose. Or was it the food?'

Carrie shrugged rather listlessly. 'I'm all right, really I am.'

'Perhaps you should take a holiday?' Miss Haversham suggested. 'You're due for a couple of weeks. Why not go off somewhere and have a good rest for a few days?'

'No, thank you,' shuddered Carrie. She couldn't think of a worse form of torture than lying on a sunny beach all day, all those empty hours with nothing to fill them except a lot of tormenting memories. 'I want to work.'

'Well, if you're sure,' shrugged Miss Haversham. 'I've an American businessman who rang this morning, he's over here to attend a conference and to visit British factories in the same line of business as his own. He brought his own secretary over with him, but unfortunately she's been rushed to hospital to have her appendix out, so he urgently needs a replacement. Are you interested?'

No, Carrie wasn't, but she took the job anyway. The American was charming and more than a little interested in her, but she skilfully fended him off, and said goodbye to him at the end of the assignment without any regrets.

There was just one bright spot in all the grey, grey days, a long and very expensive phone call to her mother in South America. They'd chatted for quite a long time about ordinary things before her mother had finally fallen silent for a few seconds.

'What is it, Carrie?' she asked bluntly at the end of the silence. 'Why have you *really* called?'

Carrie sighed softly. 'Is it that obvious?'

'Only to someone who knows you very well,' her mother answered gently. 'Is it a man?'

'Yes,' she confessed after a moment's hesitation.

'The wrong man?' probed her mother sympathetically.

'No, the right man.'

Another thoughtful silence over the thousands of miles that separated them.

'Then it's rather one-sided?'

'He—didn't want to get involved.'

'My poor love,' sympathised her mother. 'If only you weren't so far away. Look, why don't you come and stay with us for a few weeks? It'll be carnival time soon, and you know what a mad chaos that always is. It might help you to forget.'

For a moment she was sorely tempted. Then she slowly shook her head.

'No, I can't.' She tried hard to find the right words to explain. 'I know it's over, I know that he isn't going to ring me or write to me, but I still want to be here——'

'So that you'll know he isn't doing any of those things?' her mother finished for her rather wryly.

'It doesn't make sense, does it?' Carrie admitted.

'It never does,' sighed her mother. 'Love's the most inexplicable thing in the whole world.' They were both silent for several moments, then her mother continued to speak in a brisker tone. 'You know you can always fly out and join us if you get too miserable. And do ring me whenever you need to, never mind the cost. Listen, I'm afraid I must go, darling, your father's dragging me off to some frightfully boring dinner with a local industrialist and we're already late. Remember that we love you and that we're here if you need us.'

Carrie said goodbye, reluctantly replacing the receiver, then released a tiny sigh. *Why* couldn't she have accepted her mother's invitation to fly to South America? Kyle wasn't going to get in touch with her, only a fool would hang around like this, waiting and waiting for a miracle that just wasn't going to happen.

The weeks dragged by, each one somehow harder to get through than the last. Weren't things meant to improve with time? she asked herself rather desperately one morning when it was an awful effort even to drag herself out of bed; face the dreary day ahead. Surely they weren't supposed to just keep getting worse and worse? She felt an awful impulse to crawl back into bed, curl up in a small ball like an animal in pain. Instead, she put on her brightest outfit, plastered her pale face with make-up, stuck a fancy clip in her limp hair. She was getting to be a master of disguise, she acknowledged with some bitterness. And why the hell not? The pain inside her was very private, she didn't intend to advertise to the whole world how very badly hurt she'd been. One thing she definitely couldn't cope with right now was a lot of suffocating sympathy. That would just about push her into the breakdown she was so grimly determined to avoid.

At the agency, Miss Haversham was waiting for her with a new assignment.

'You already know him,' she announced brightly. 'Sir Charles Kingwood. He's asked for you especially.'

Carrie's head shot up.

'Sir Charles?' she echoed incredulously.

'He seems to think you'd be ideal for this job. Apparently he owns a large house in Kent, surrounded by acres of ground which he plans to turn into a safari park. He's already appointed a manager to set the whole thing up, but he needs a temporary secretary for the manager, a couple of weeks, he thinks, maybe three. They've already advertised for a permanent girl, but they need someone to fill in while they sort through the applications and set up the interviews. What do you think?'

'I don't want to work for Sir Charles,' Carrie stated bluntly.

'But you won't be,' Miss Haversham assured her. 'I've already explained, you'll be working for the manager. You probably won't see much of Sir Charles, he's got so many business interests that this safari park's really only a small sideline. Won't you give it a try, Carrie? It sounds quite interesting.'

On the point of insisting that Miss Haversham find another girl for this assignment, Carrie suddenly sighed listlessly. She didn't really care if she went to work for Sir Charles or not. These days nothing seemed particularly important, the days and nights were just a long, dreary succession of hours that somehow had to be got through, and working hard was the only thing that kept her sane, helped to fill the endless emptiness.

Early the next morning, she drove down to Kent, having little trouble in finding the large, handsome, red-brick house set in a fold of the hills. To her surprise, Sir Charles himself was waiting at the entrance to greet her.

'I'm very glad you've come,' he smiled gravely. 'I was afraid you wouldn't after—well, after the rather stupid way I behaved in Africa.'

She gave a small shrug. 'You only did what you thought was right.'

'Perhaps,' he agreed. 'But a little late in life, I'm beginning to realise that my daughter must be allowed to live her own life, make her own mistakes. I suppose that by bringing you here, I'm trying in my rather inadequate way to make amends.'

Carrie didn't have the slightest idea what he was talking about, but since she wasn't really interested, she followed him into the house without bothering to ask any questions. He led her through a large, beautifully furnished entrance hall, then along a passage that led to the back of the house. Finally, he stopped and opened a door.

'This will be your office,' he told her. 'It's all rather makeshift at the moment, I'm afraid, everything's in the planning stages right now. If you'd like to make yourself at home, I'll tell the general manager you've arrived.'

She wandered around the office, examined the electric typewriter without much interest, then walked over to the window and stared out at the beautiful garden.

Since she had her back to the door, she didn't see it open silently and a tall figure come in. A tiny shiver danced up her spine, though, touched the nape of her neck with a brief chill and, with a sense of dread, she very slowly turned round.

Kyle was standing just, a few feet away, very still, very tense, his gaze fixed on her with almost terrifying intensity. She drew in a sharp breath. He looked pale, strained, as if he'd had many sleepless nights since she'd last seen him.

'I—I didn't expect *you* to be here,' she somehow managed to stutter at last. 'Are you——' She fought desperately for control of her voice, somehow regained it. 'Are you staying with Sir Charles?' she asked in a much steadier tone. Yet inside her nerves were still thrashing around, completely out of control.

'Not staying with him—working for him,' he answered tersely.

She blinked dazedly. 'I don't understand.'

He came a little further into the room and she instinctively drew back, frightened of letting him come any nearer, certain he would see her wildly pounding pulses, the convulsive trembling of her limbs. With a small growl, he spun away from her, threw himself into a chair on the far side of the room.

'Sir Charles offered me a job and I accepted it,' he told her, his gaze swivelling back to fix on her again, as if he had a compulsive need to look at her, constantly reassure himself that she was actually there. 'I'm going to set up and run this safari park he's planning.'

Astonishment flooded her. '*You're* the general manager?'

He nodded. 'That's right.'

'I don't believe it,' she stated bluntly. 'You'd hate a job like this. You couldn't stand being tied down in one place, having to take orders from someone else instead of making all your own decisions.'

'What I can't stand is being apart from you,' he answered softly. And while she was still digesting that incredible remark, he went on, 'And the job should be very interesting. Sir Charles wants all the usual big crowd-pullers, lions and tigers and elephants, but I've got other plans. I want to set up a breeding programme for some of the species that are in danger of becoming extinct. I think the public response should be good, people are becoming increasingly interested in the pre-servation of wild-life, and——'

'Kyle, stop it!' she burst out, unable to listen to him one moment longer.

He looked slightly bewildered. 'I thought you'd be interested in hearing about my plans.'

'I am. But I want you to tell me what your next documentary's going to be, what books you're planning, not—not that you're going to abandon everything and run some fancy zoo!'

His features hardened, his eyes blazed. 'I've made my decision, Carrie, and I intend to stick to it.' He buried his fingers deep into his shaggy black hair, exhaled deeply, as if fighting hard to keep his temper. 'Listen,' he went on in a much quieter, more controlled tone, 'when I came back from that hospital check-up and found you'd gone, I was angry—very, very angry. I wanted to come roaring after you, drag you straight back to the lodge again. Then I realised how totally selfish I was being. After all, what was I dragging you back to? A life that's constantly unsettled, no permanent home, no proper social life. No woman could be expected to put up with that. So I told myself I'd just have to learn how to live without you. I couldn't do it, though. Don't ask me why the hell not, I can't explain it. I simply woke up one morning and knew that nothing I did was ever going to have any meaning any more if you weren't there to share it. And that was when I realised that I was going to have to make some major changes in my life.'

Carrie's legs had gone peculiarly weak and she had to lean against the wall behind her to keep herself upright.

'So that's when you decided to take this job with Sir Charles?' she asked shakily.

Kyle nodded.

'He'd already offered it to me once before, but I'd turned him down. I went to him and asked if the offer was still open, and he said it was. There was a lot of straight talking on both sides—among other things, I told him that Lydia wasn't included in the deal, that he'd have to forget any plans he had for the two of us getting married. Once he'd accepted that, everything was fairly straight-forward. He agreed to give me a virtually free hand in setting up this place, and we flew back to England to finalise the arrangements.'

Carrie stood up straight as she found she no longer needed the support of the wall.

'Well, the two of you seem to have planned out my life very nicely,' she remarked with a touch of sarcasm. 'I suppose the idea is that we set up home together in a little cottage on the estate, then live happily ever after?'

'Not exactly,' growled Kyle. 'I had it in mind to get married first.'

And that knocked the breath right out of her, she actually gasped out loud. Marriage to Kyle—the impossible dream was suddenly within her grasp. Then a surge of indignation welled up again, wiping out the brief moment of disbelieving joy.

'I suppose it never occurred to either of you to ask what *I* wanted,' she retorted. 'I was just expected to fall in with your plans like a mindless dummy!'

One black eyebrow shot up.

'I don't think anyone's ever likely to accuse you

of being mindless,' he commented drily. 'You're one of the most contrary, independent females I've ever encountered.' Then his face altered radically, the silver eyes seemed to lose much of their brightness. 'You don't want to marry me?' he asked, a queer note of uncertainty creeping into his voice.

'I want to marry you more than anything else in the world,' she admitted shakily, feeling her bones begin to melt at the sudden light that flared in his eyes. 'What I *don't* want,' she added warningly, 'is for you to give up your career.'

He leapt to his feet, prowled restlessly around the room. 'Look, I ruined one marriage because I refused to make any compromises, I don't want to risk that happening again. This is a big enough gamble as it is, I'm not the easiest man in the world to live with, I know that. That's why we've got to give this marriage every possible chance.'

Stubbornly, she stood her ground. 'If you want to marry me, you've got to give up this mad idea of running a safari park. You'll loathe every minute of it, and we'll both end up completely miserable.'

He was staring at her now in blank disbelief. 'Don't you *want* a settled home?' he demanded incredulously.

Carrie suddenly felt the need to sit down. There was a window-seat behind her and she collapsed into it.

'Will you tell me something?' she asked, looking up at him.

He hesitated, then gave an abrupt nod.

'All right,' she said, drawing in a deep breath. 'What were you planning to do for the next year or so? I mean, before you suddenly got it into your head that getting married meant giving it all up?'

His mouth set into a familiar, stubborn line. 'There's not much point in talking about it now.'

'Tell me!' she insisted.

'Well—actually I was thinking of doing a series on the truly primitive cultures of the world. They're disappearing so fast, being wiped out by the relentless march of so-called civilisation—I think it's very important to make a film record while it's still possible.' Enthusiasm gathered in his voice, the silver-grey eyes became suddenly vitally alive. 'It would mean travelling to some of the most inaccessible places on earth, of course, and it would probably take a couple of years to complete, maybe even longer. Afterwards, there'd be a book to write, to accompany the series, and I'd plans for another book on——'

He abruptly broke off, gave a tiny, resigned shrug of his shoulders. Carrie saw it, impulsively jumped to her feet and went over to him.

'Now ask me what *I* want to do for the next few years,' she instructed, meeting and holding his gaze.

He stared down into her sapphire eyes, then his hands involuntarily moved upwards, clamped themselves around her waist in a possessive gesture.

'What do you want, Carrie?' he asked in a quiet yet rather shaken voice.

'I want to come with you, wherever you go,' she answered without hesitation. 'Kyle, I've been travelling around all my life and I love it. We're two of a kind, don't you know that? We've both got gypsy blood in our veins, we're never going to be happy staying in the same place for the rest of our lives. Let's do your series on the primitive cultures. Then we'll come back to England and you can write your book and I can have a baby. And after that, we'll find somewhere else to wander off to. There must be a thousand interesting places in the world that neither of us have seen yet.'

'You're crazy,' he said wonderingly. 'Quite, quite crazy. And what would we do with this baby when we go wandering off again?'

'Take it with us, of course,' she answered calmly. 'Babies are pretty tough, you know. My parents hauled me halfway round the world when I was young, and I survived perfectly well. There's no reason why our children shouldn't do the same thing. Or if we're going somewhere really remote, we'll find a nanny who'll cosset and love it until we get back again, because I'm never going to let you go anywhere without me.'

His fingers had begun moving purposefully, curling round the curve of her breast in a familiar way that made her gasp suddenly. Yet there was still a slight note of hesitation in his voice as he spoke.

'Are you sure about this, Carrie? Absolutely sure?'

'If I'd wanted security and a husband who worked nine to five, I could have married Sir Charles,' she teased. 'After all, he's very eligible and quite distinguished-looking.'

His grip tightened, his thumb brushing over her hardening nipple in a loving caress.

'You're going to marry me,' he ordered roughly.

'It looks like it,' she agreed demurely. 'Although you haven't told me yet *why* you want to marry me.'

He stared at her in astonishment.

'Because I love you, damn it! I love you,' he added in a very different tone of voice.

She sighed contentedly. 'I thought you were never going to say it.'

'Witch!' he accused with tender amusement. He drew her closer, fitted her to the curves of his body, his breath quickening slightly. 'It's funny,' he muttered rather unsteadily, 'but I already know exactly how it feels when you touch me, how sweet your hands feel on my body. After you'd left the lodge, it drove me nearly crazy night after night. I kept remembering, wanting—I could even see your beautiful nakedness—I thought I was going completely mad.'

She buried her face against his shoulder.

'Don't you remember anything that happened while you were sick with that fever in the Maasai village?' she asked a little shyly.

'I seem to recall having some incredibly erotic dreams,' he said slowly. 'It must have been something in those herbs they gave me——' He broke off, his voice roughening with suspicion. 'They weren't dreams?' he challenged incredulously. 'It actually happened? But surely I didn't——?'

'No, you didn't,' she agreed with a grin. 'As a matter of fact, you fell asleep at the vital moment.'

He threw back his head and laughed in disbelief.

'That won't happen again,' he promised, and for an instant he held her tight agains his throbbing body, making the breath catch lightly in her throat.

'I've a cottage not far from here,' he told her with sudden urgency. 'It's my retreat, the place I go when I want complete privacy. We could be there in an hour.'

'Shouldn't you tell Sir Charles that you're not going to take his job?' she reminded him gently.

'We'll phone him later—much later,' came his husky response.

'Perhaps even tomorrow,' she murmured.

'Or the day after,' he breathed, his tongue lightly flicking over the soft outline of her lips, his mouth brushing against hers with a tantalising promise of the thousand and one pleasures that lay ahead of them.

She melted against him, shared the flame that flared between them.

'I think we'd better leave right now,' he reluctantly muttered a few minutes later, 'while I'm still in a fit state to drive.'

She laughed softly, then linked her hand with his, and they silently left the house together, walking through the golden sunlight towards a future that was bright with promise.

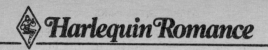 **Harlequin Romance**

Coming Next Month

2839 ODD MAN OUT Sharron Cohen
A chauffeur's daughter's hand in marriage is priceless—both to
her fiancé and to his estranged brother, her first great love.
Would he use that love just to give his rival a run for his money?

2840 FOR KARIN'S SAKE Samantha Day
A young widow is just beginning to feel whole again when
her heart goes out to a troubled child and her uncompromising
father. But is he suggesting marriage—just for the sake of
his daughter?

2841 THE MARATI LEGACY Dana James
Although she's still haunted by the pain of a past experience, an
oceanographer joins a search for sunken treasure off the
Madagascar coast. She finds adventure, but she also finds
love—and is frightened by its intensity.

2842 IMMUNE TO LOVE Claudia Jameson
No one is immune to love. But when a career girl falls for her
charming boss, she's afraid she'll contract permanent
heartache. Unless she can discover why he suddenly pulls away
from her...

2843 RING OF CLADDAGH Annabel Murray
Claddagh Hall is left jointly to a London fashion designer and
the rightful heir, a provocative and teasing Irishman. But it's no
joking matter when he proposes marriage!

2844 MOROCCAN MADNESS Angela Wells
After their whirlwind courtship, her Moroccan husband
accused her of betraying him on their wedding night. Now he
wants her back. To continue the madness that drove her away?
Or to rekindle the love that still smolders between them?

Available in June wherever paperback books are sold, or
through Harlequin Reader Service.

In the U.S.
901 Fuhrmann Blvd.
P.O. Box 1397
Buffalo, N.Y. 14240-1397

In Canada
P.O. Box 603
Fort Erie, Ontario
L2A 5X3

ATTRACTIVE, SPACE SAVING BOOK RACK

Display your most prized novels on this handsome and sturdy book rack. The hand-rubbed walnut finish will blend into your library decor with quiet elegance, providing a practical organizer for your favorite hard-or soft-covered books.

Only $9.95

Approximately 16" x 8" when assembled

Assembles in seconds!

To order, rush your name, address and zip code, along with a check or money order for $10.70* ($9.95 plus 75¢ postage and handling) payable to *Harlequin Reader Service*:

Harlequin Reader Service
Book Rack Offer
901 Fuhrmann Blvd.
P.O. Box 1396
Buffalo, NY 14269-1396

Offer not available in Canada.

BKR-1A

*New York and Iowa residents add appropriate sales tax.

Janet Dailey
Americana

A romantic tour of America with
Janet Dailey!

Enjoy two releases each month from this
collection of your favorite previously
published Janet Dailey titles, presented
alphabetically state by state.

Available NOW wherever paperback books
are sold.

JDA-B-1

**For the millions who can't read
Give the Gift of Literacy**

One out of five adults in North America
cannot read or write well enough
to fill out a job application
or understand the directions on a bottle of medicine.

**You can change all this by joining the fight
against illiteracy.**

For more information write to:
Contact, Box 81826, Lincoln, Neb. 68501
In the United States, call toll free: 800-228-3225

**The only degree you need
is a degree of caring**

"This ad made possible with the cooperation of the Coalition for Literacy and the Ad Council."
Give the Gift of Literacy Campaign is a project of the book and periodical industry,
in partnership with Telephone Pioneers of America.

LIT—A—1